"Trying to get rid of me?"

Charlotte was startled, but then saw the twinkle in Paul's eye. Still, she couldn't resist adding one more thing.

"I hope I've made it clear, Paul, I won't tolerate being pressured about this. But at the same time, I want you to trust me. Can you do that? I care about Tyson, too, just as I care about all of my students."

"I trust you," Paul said, but the words seemed unfamiliar in his mouth. "I, uh, missed you at lunch yesterday," he added, his tone gruff with confession.

So he had noticed. *I missed you, too...*

But she couldn't bring herself to say the words or to stir the embers.

She suddenly wondered how it would go over if she was to start dating the guardian of one of her students.

Whoa, now, where had that thought come from?

Besides, there was her application, making its way through the mail and waiting to bring back with it the answer to her future.

An answer that she was no longer sure she was ready for.

Donna Gartshore loves reading and writing. She also writes short stories, poetry and devotionals. She often veers off to the book section in the grocery store when she should be buying food. Besides talking about books and writing, Donna loves spending time with her daughter, Sunday family suppers and engaging online with the writing community.

Books by Donna Gartshore

Love Inspired

Instant Family
Instant Father

Visit the Author Profile page at Harlequin.com.

Instant Father

Donna Gartshore

HARLEQUIN® LOVE INSPIRED®

Recycling programs for this product may not exist in your area.

LOVE INSPIRED BOOKS

ISBN-13: 978-1-335-53914-4

Instant Father

www.Harlequin.com

Printed in U.S.A.

And he said unto me, My grace is sufficient
for thee: for my strength is made perfect in
weakness. Most gladly therefore will I
rather glory in my infirmities, that
the power of Christ may rest upon me.

—*2 Corinthians* 12:9

This book is, as always, for my daughter,
who brings light and fun to my days.

For my family, who supports me
and believes in me.

And for my writing group and other friends,
who keep me encouraged.

Thanks again to Melissa Endlich
for helping me to be the best writer I can be.

Chapter One

It was Friday in the second week of September, her grade-one students, restless and energetic, had departed for the weekend and Charlotte Connelly was intently focused on her computer screen. But instead of looking at lesson plans, she studied pictures of people engaged in overseas missionary work. During the community activities on Wednesday night at her church, where Charlotte often assisted with literacy volunteer work, one of the other volunteers had pointed out the opportunity to her and said he thought she would be perfect for it.

Since then, Charlotte hadn't been able to focus on anything but the thought of going overseas. There was no doubt she was ready for a change, perhaps even for some adventure. But would she actually dare to do it?

She had lived in Green Valley, a small community about a forty-minute drive from Regina, Saskatchewan, her entire life. At age twenty-five, she was still single, and she didn't see that changing anytime soon.

The volunteers looked happy and fulfilled in a way that she hadn't felt for a long time. Well, truthfully, not since Anna... But as soon as the thought of her younger sister came into her mind, it was immediately followed by guilt-ridden memories that blamed her for what happened. She knew that her parents counted on her, especially since her mother was unwell these days. Charlotte suspected it was stress, but the headaches and upset stomach were real and debilitating.

But Charlotte still had the longing in her heart to have a life that brought her true fulfillment...maybe even love. But, despite being a believer and a regular churchgoer, she didn't feel like she knew what His intentions were for her life. Was this opportunity to do missionary work a nudge toward discovering this?

A soft clearing of a throat from the classroom doorway startled Charlotte. She quickly regained her composure and turned on her professional smile before seeing who it was. Then her smile wavered for a moment, as something unsettling flowed through her, an odd mix of disturbing and pleasant. A moment later, the sensation was gone and she was left feeling slightly shell-shocked.

She couldn't explain why she'd had such a visceral reaction to seeing Paul Belvedere standing in the classroom doorway. He was the uncle and guardian of one of her students, Tyson Francis, and he wasn't the only parent or guardian to seek her out lately.

Although, admittedly, she couldn't recall any other class parents who filled up the doorway with such broad shoulders and whose dark brown eyes were so intense.

"I hope I'm not interrupting," Paul said in the deep voice that several women in town gossiped about. "I—uh—Mildred Price said it was no trouble if I picked Tyson up late today, so I thought I'd take the opportunity to…" For a split second Charlotte saw weariness and uncertainty wash across Paul's strong-boned face. Then he cleared his throat again and said in a forthright way, "I want to talk to you about how Tyson is doing and I want you to be honest with me."

"Yes, of course, Mr. Belvedere," Charlotte said. "Please come in and have a seat."

She couldn't help noting that the chair she kept by her desk for this purpose was dwarfed by his size. Yet what should have been a comical picture only served to emphasize his physique.

Stop it, Charlotte, she scolded herself.

She knew that Paul's question wasn't a casual one. Even if she hadn't been Tyson's teacher, it would have been impossible in a town the size of Green Valley to avoid knowledge of the tragedy.

Tyson and his parents, Ross and Erica Francis, had only been living in town for a couple of years, yet they'd readily fit in. One fateful night, about seven months ago, Ross and Erica left Tyson with a babysitter and drove into Regina for dinner and a movie. They never made it to the movie. As they were crossing the street after dinner, they were struck down by a drunk driver and killed instantly.

Tyson had woken up to the news that he would never see his parents again.

Charlotte swallowed hard and reminded herself that Paul had come to get her opinion on his nephew, not to watch her dissolve in a puddle of sympathy, even if she did understand all too well what it was like to lose a sister. But that was something she never talked about.

He shifted in the small chair, and she realized that he was waiting for her to answer his question. There was something edgy about him, not dangerous, but as if he didn't have time to waste.

"I'm glad that you came to talk to me," Charlotte said. "I've actually been thinking about whether I should contact you, but I wanted to give it some time. In some ways Tyson is doing as well as can be expected. All children experience an adjustment period between kindergarten and grade one because of the full days and higher expectations, and, of course with Tyson…"

A shadow passed through Paul's eyes, and his jaw tightened, so she rapidly stepped around the emotional land mine.

"We'll just say that Tyson has some additional challenges."

Paul gave a grim nod. "So he's having problems? I was afraid of that."

Charlotte thought about Tyson and pictured his unruly mop of reddish hair, the dash of freckles across his nose and his smile, which, though infrequent, was gap-toothed and endearing.

"Tyson is a sweet boy," she said with sincerity. "He's kindhearted and smart and, given time, I know he'll be fine."

She silently prayed that her confident prediction would come true.

"But…" Paul prompted.

"But in the meantime I do think he could use some extra assistance and attention."

"What are you suggesting?" Paul asked.

"I'm saying that we have to work as a team. We both care about Tyson and are committed to helping him through this. We can't bring back his parents." Charlotte swallowed briefly then braced herself. She couldn't give in to emotion now. "But if we work together, I know we can make a difference for him."

Paul appeared to be considering her words, then he asked, "What about the other kids? How is Tyson getting along with them?"

"Social interactions are an adjustment for all of the children," she said cautiously. "It's really not that long since their only social interactions were with their parents."

She stopped herself. But it was Paul who pushed past the hard moment in the conversation.

"Is Tyson not getting along with the other children?" he asked.

"He's a friendly and kind little boy," Charlotte reiterated. "But again, there are struggles, for obvious reasons. He has one or two friends that he seems to be comfortable with, but he still likes to be alone much of the time."

"And you think we should be concerned?" Paul asked sharply.

Charlotte was momentarily flustered by his tone, then regained her composure. It was only natural that Paul would be uptight. Not only was he new to town, but she'd heard that he was also a confirmed bachelor. Parenting was new to him. Plus he'd also be dealing with his own grief over his sister.

"I think it's all part of the struggle he's going through," Charlotte said. "I do want to say again that I think Tyson is doing quite well, but it's going to take both of us, as well as the support of the community, to keep him on the path to healing."

Again Paul scrutinized her in a way that made Charlotte feel like he could see right through her. Then his face relaxed and he said. "Okay, thank you for answering all of my questions, Ms. Connelly."

"That's what I'm here for," Charlotte said. "I'll keep in close touch with you about Tyson's progress and trust you'll do the same for me. Also, Mr. Belvedere, I know that you've had a loss, too. Green Valley is a supportive community—don't be afraid to reach out."

"Thanks, I appreciate it." But Paul's face

had gone stony, discouraging further discussion on the matter. He glanced at his watch and unfolded himself out of the chair. Charlotte stood up to walk out of the room with him, noticing that, although she was five feet seven inches, she felt tiny beside him. She tried not to feel like a little girl as she scrambled to match his long stride.

Although Paul had indicated that he was satisfied with her answers, Charlotte felt like there was something he wasn't saying, and she wanted to offer more reassurance, but she didn't know how.

Dear Lord, help me to help Tyson and his uncle. Show me what I can do.

Almost immediately, the community activities that took place at Green Valley Community Church on Wednesday nights came to mind.

"Listen, Paul," she said, tilting her face up to catch his eye.

He stopped walking and looked down at her, waiting.

"You may already know this, but there are a variety of activities that take place at the Green Valley church on Wednesday nights. It would be a great way for Tyson to have more bonding time with his classmates and a chance for you to get to know more people, too. I'm usually with the literacy volunteer group and—"

"Thank you," Paul said. "Sorry to interrupt, but I do need to get going. I promised Mildred and Tyson that I wouldn't be too late. Maybe we'll drop by the church—we'll see."

But Charlotte didn't have confidence that they would. She had never seen them there on a Sunday morning.

As they reached the exit, they almost ran into Rena Acoose, who was heading back into the school with a fretful look in her beautiful dark eyes.

"Rena, what's the matter?" Charlotte asked. Her First Nations friend was the grade-four teacher at Parkside Elementary School. "I thought you were long gone."

"That was the plan," Rena said rather breathlessly. "I have the car today because I'm supposed to be getting a few groceries after work, but it won't start. I left my cell phone in my desk and I need to get hold of Seth."

Her husband owned and managed the local coffee and bakeshop, Seth's Café, a popular hangout on Main Street.

"It's just been one thing after another," Rena said, shaking her head. "I know we'll have to get a mechanic to look at it, but we just found out that we have to get a new furnace installed before winter, too."

"I could take a look," Paul said, and Charlotte remembered that he'd been hired as a mechanic by Mildred's brother, Harold. Harold said Paul did high-quality work.

"I have to pick up Ty right now, but I could stop by Harold's Garage and grab my tools and come back to have a look."

Rena shook her head. "That's so nice of you," she said. "But I really can't afford it right now."

"Oh, I'm sure we can work something out," Paul said. "Maybe just mention to Seth that Tyson and I are pretty fond of that bannock he makes."

Paul's half smile caused Charlotte's cheeks to flush. More than his obvious good looks, she was attracted to his willingness to help. Her curiosity was piqued.

A moment later, though, she tamped down on the curiosity. Her only goal with him was to help his nephew, although it did no harm to notice how handsome he was.

Paul departed with a promise to return to look at Rena's car. As soon as he was out of earshot, Charlotte felt her friend's fingers eagerly gripping her forearm.

"He's cute!" Rena whispered dramatically. "A nice guy, too. And don't even try to pretend you haven't noticed."

Wanting to steer Rena away from any matchmaking thoughts, Charlotte said, "I've been looking online at sites about overseas missionary work."

"Do you think you'll do it?" Rena asked.

"I'm not sure. I mean, I'd really like to, but…there's a lot to think about."

Rena nodded.

One of the best things about longtime friends, Charlotte thought, was that you didn't have to spell everything out for them.

"You headed to your parents' tonight," Rena said. It wasn't a question. Everyone who knew Charlotte knew that she went to her parents' on Friday evenings for tea and shortbread and a game of cribbage with her father.

"Yes, I keep telling Mom that they can come to my place if she's not up to it," Charlotte said. "Or we can take a night off, but she says she likes doing it. I guess…well, I guess she likes knowing that some things won't change."

But, as she left Rena at the school to wait for Paul to look at her car, Charlotte wondered what Paul Belvedere did on a Friday night.

* * *

Could he trust Ms. Connelly to do everything she could for Tyson? Paul wondered if she would truly pay enough attention, because he was all too aware of what could happen when teachers—and parents—let things slip through the cracks.

Despite himself, he was also trying to decide if she was pretty. His first reaction was that she was plain, until he caught a glimpse of her eyes. They were quite extraordinary, violet with long thick lashes, and they brought an unexpected beauty to her face. She was tall and slim and her straight-line gray skirt and pink blouse made him think of a prim librarian. She had light brown hair that she wore pulled back in a low ponytail, her nose was small and straight, her mouth was on the wide side and she didn't wear lipstick.

Not that any of that mattered. The important thing was how Tyson felt about her and, so far, he said he liked her. Plus Paul had heard nothing but good things around town about Ms. Connelly.

Mildred Price lived one block over from Main Street, and as Paul headed toward her house, he passed the few businesses in town—Seth's Café, Fran's Women's Wear and Dudley's Pharmacy. It still bemused him that he could walk from one end of Main Street to the other in less time than it took him to pick up one of Seth's renowned cups of coffee. It was a real change from Toronto, which was the last place he'd lived.

His sister, Erica, had emailed him about Green Valley, and he'd teased her, unable to believe they would last for long there. She and her husband, Ross, were city people through and through, or so he had thought. But they'd wanted to raise Tyson in a place where he could play outdoors and where they would actually know their neighbors' names. Despite how much he'd enjoyed giving his older sister a hard time, Paul had been happy to be proven wrong, because Erica and her family had thrived in Green Valley.

He still had a hard time believing they were gone. Somehow, he would get through it, one step at a time. He would pick up Tyson. He would stop by the garage and grab his tools. He would look at Rena's car. Tyson liked Rena and wouldn't mind hanging out while Paul did his work. One step at a time, he could do this.

Paul always felt reassured at Mildred's home. Everything about her freshly painted house and immaculately tended yard spelled comfort and order to him. He regretted the time that Tyson had to spend with a caregiver, but since it was necessary, he was glad that Ty was happy there.

Mildred had never married and had no children of her own, but she was an honorary grandmother to the entire town. In contrast with her house and yard that conjured images of a storybook grandmother, Mildred was six feet tall, broad-shouldered and wore overalls and her white hair was always in two long braids.

The front door of her house swung open as Paul neared it. Clearly, they were watching for him.

"How did Tyson get along today?" Paul asked Mildred as his nephew was getting his backpack.

"Oh, he's always a good boy," Mildred said in her soft, sweet voice. "How was your meeting with his teacher? Charlotte Connelly is a fine young woman."

Was it his imagination, or did the older woman put extra emphasis on her statement about Charlotte?

"She seems like a good teacher," Paul said cautiously. He had no desire to delve any deeper into the topic. Charlotte Connelly was not his type. Not that he'd ever really had a type. Dating had never been a priority for him.

Survival had.

Now he had one goal, and that was to be the best guardian possible for Tyson. Even though he was sure Erica would never have named him guardian if she'd known how unstable his faith was now.

"Thanks for letting Tyson stay late," Paul said.

"My pleasure," Mildred said.

"We have to stop by Harold's for a couple of minutes," Paul explained to Tyson as they went down the sidewalk together. "Then I'm going to have a quick look at Ms. Acoose's car."

"I like her," Tyson declared.

"I thought you did," Paul nodded. "You like your teacher, Ms. Connelly, too, don't you?"

Tyson nodded. "Yup." Paul waited to hear more, but Tyson had already moved on to the subject of his after-school snack. It amused Paul, the way the boy's thoughts could drift from one topic to another like scattered fluff from a dandelion wish.

"We had oatmeal and raisin cookies," Tyson said. "Except not raisins, because Mildred knows I don't like raisins."

"I don't like raisins, either," Paul said.

Tyson looked up at him with those large blue eyes of his and nodded with a satisfied sigh. The expression on his freckled face clearly said that they were two men bonding over a shared dislike of wrinkled fruit.

It was these moments that gave Paul hope that he could do this. He could do this whole guardian, raise-a-child-into-a-responsible-adult thing.

"Did my mom and dad like raisins?" Tyson asked. "Is there snacks in Heaven? Do you haveta have raisins?"

And, just like that, the cautiously emerging confidence was gone, like a rabbit being chased away by hounds.

Paul didn't know how he felt about the God and Heaven questions these days. In Paul's opinion, He had been pretty much MIA during Paul's school days, and then after losing Erica… Well, how was he supposed to feel about a God who would allow all of that?

But there was a little boy, wide eyes fixed on him, waiting for an answer, and he couldn't confess his raging doubts to anyone, let alone a six-year-old who counted on him.

"I'm sure you only eat what you like in Heaven," he finally answered. To Paul's great relief, there were no more questions. As they walked to Harold's Garage, Tyson chatted about the things he had learned in Ms. Connelly's class that week. Each time he said her name, Paul was unwittingly struck by a vision of her violet eyes.

They reached the garage, and Harold greeted Tyson in the booming voice that the little boy loved.

"Why, hello, good sir! And what brings you my way? Do you need a part for your car? Or have you come to help me organize my wrenches?"

Tyson giggled, then suppressed it because that was part of the game.

"I've come to buy a racing car, good sir." He did his best to imitate the low boom in Harold's voice, and Paul broke into a grin.

Harold Price was five years younger and a good six inches shorter than his sister, Mildred, but his warm blue eyes matched hers and, although he was married and had a family of his own, he cared equally about Green Valley and the people who lived there.

"I'm actually here to get my tools," Paul said. "I promised someone a favor."

Harold considered that briefly, then nodded. Paul knew the older man was an astute businessman but that he would also understand that being a Good Samaritan was beneficial to everyone in the long run.

"Since you're here," Harold said. "There is something I'd like to talk to you about."

He reached down and lifted Tyson up, swinging him onto a high stool behind a workbench.

"Mind the shop, good sir?" he asked. "I'm just going to have a quick chat with your uncle."

Tyson sat up straight and proud. "You got it, good sir," he replied.

Paul felt the relaxed, enjoyable feeling of the moment slip away into apprehension. But he quickly reasoned that he was a good mechanic and he knew he worked hard.

Back in Harold's office, a small room crammed with a desk, one chair and shelves filled top to bottom with binders and stacks of paper, Harold indicated that Paul should sit.

"This won't take long," Harold promised. "First off, you're a fine mechanic, Paul. I don't know if I've worked with a better one."

"Thank you," Paul said, feeling the thread of tension in his shoulders begin to unravel.

"However…"

The thread pulled taut again.

"Competition in this business is fierce," Harold continued. "Sure, folks will come here because they know us and it's convenient. But there are garages being set up all over the place, so it's very important that we offer excellent customer service."

He leaned forward, linking his hands together and studying Paul's face intently. "Do you understand what I'm saying?"

Paul couldn't think of a single time when he'd done less than his best work. "I'm not sure I do."

"You do great work," Harold reiterated, "and the customers do like you. It's just that…" He stopped, looking as if it pained him to say what he had to say. "Mrs. Meissner had a bit of a complaint about you yesterday."

"A complaint?" Paul repeated, trying to think of his dealings with her. He had fixed her car, which hadn't been an easy job. Also, in the short time he'd known Mrs. Meissner, she struck him a chronic complainer.

"Maybe *complaint* is too strong a word," Harold amended. "Let's say she had a concern about you."

"What was it?" Paul asked, wishing that his boss would get to the point. He didn't want to leave Tyson waiting too long.

"Well, she always likes someone to review her invoices with her," Harold explained, "and she said that you refused to do it." Harold looked at him, as if sure there was a logical explanation.

Suddenly Paul remembered the incident. Mrs. Meissner had said something about a price being higher than usual. Paul had remarked that inflation seemed to impact everything and then had gone into the shop to let the next customer know he was ready for him.

His mind raced, like a mouse going through a maze after some elusive cheese. He would have to apologize and give some kind of reason. He had to make sure that he bonded with the people of this town, for Tyson's sake, even if his own inclination was to run away as soon as the pressure was on. Maybe he would take Ms. Connelly up on her offer of Ty and him joining in those Wednesday night activities at church.

There was only one thing he was sure of. There was no absolutely no way he could tell Harold, or Mrs. Meissner, or anyone else that the reason he hadn't reviewed the invoice with her was because he couldn't read.

Chapter Two

Late Saturday morning, Charlotte was sitting with her cousin Bridget at Seth's Café.
As always, the place was busy, and Seth was
cooking, calling out orders and chatting with
the customers. His black hair spiked out in all
directions, regardless of what he was doing
but, inevitably, one of the regulars was bound
to call out, "Look at Seth, he's working so
hard his hair's standing on end!"

The familiar joke, as well as the coffee,
lightly flavored with nutmeg, and an order
of pancakes usually soothed Charlotte, but
she had a restlessness that she couldn't quell.

Sometimes she liked to imagine different
directions her life could take. She loved music
and poetry and she'd always been fascinated
by history. Of course she could teach about
those things, but that wasn't the same thing

as actually experiencing them. Maybe one day she would travel more, go to concerts and shows and see first-hand some of the things she'd only read about.

But she had also made a promise to the uncle of a grieving little boy...

Charlotte's father and Bridget's father were brothers, both businessmen who commuted daily to Regina. Less than a year apart— Charlotte ten months older, almost to the day—she and Bridget had always been close. They were more like sisters than cousins. People always told them they looked like sisters, too, although Bridget's eyes were more denim than violet blue, and her hair was a shade lighter.

"So, what do you think?" Charlotte asked Bridget, having filled her in on her possible mission work. Bridget hadn't been at church on Wednesday night because she was on a date. Since they'd been teenagers, she and Bridget had shared their ideas of what their perfect lives would look like. Marriage and family were definitely part of the plan.

"I don't know, Char," Bridget said, twirling a piece of toast through an egg yolk. "I can't imagine you going so far away. You've never even left Saskatchewan. How are you going to handle living thousands of miles away?"

"Maybe it's time to change all that," Charlotte said quietly.

Bridget shrugged. "Maybe," she said. She finished the rest of the food on her plate and sighed. "That was *so* good, but I am not going to eat anything else until supper time." She looked around the café. "It's busy this morning."

"It always is," Charlotte said. She accepted that the conversation about missionary work was over for now. She knew that Bridget would miss her terribly if she went away, even if she had a hard time saying it.

"Who's sitting in the back corner?" Bridget asked in a lowered voice. "Don't make it obvious that you're looking."

Charlotte laughed and turned around to look. "If they're strangers here," she said to Bridget, "I won't be the first person to stare."

She briefly took in the sight of a woman who looked like she was in her early to mid-thirties, with a tired face and a distant gaze, and a boy, who looked to be about six or seven, listlessly pushing a toy car back and forth across the table.

Charlotte turned back to Bridget. "I've seen them on Wednesday nights at church, so they must live somewhere close by, but I haven't seen them Sunday and the little boy isn't at our school."

"They don't look like they feel at home here," Bridget observed.

"Maybe we should do something to make them feel welcome, then," Charlotte suggested. But she had no idea how to do that.

She felt a bit ashamed at her relief when the strangers got up to leave.

Seth sped around the café, refilling coffee mugs and water glasses. He had hired Eugenie Tyler, a high school senior, to help out in the café, but Seth still liked to mingle with his customers.

Charlotte thought with amusement that when Eugenie tried to keep up with Seth, she looked like a fledging bird in a nest watching an eagle swoop around her. But she was always pleasant and worked hard.

She also thought that it was a good thing that Seth's wife, Rena, was quiet and generally unflappable. It not only made her an effective teacher, it also provided the perfect balance for Seth's boundless energy.

Charlotte believed that there was a perfect match for everyone, at least in theory. Unfortunately, she hadn't yet met her perfect match.

Inexplicably, she pictured Paul Belvedere's deep brown eyes and the way he had studied her face as if he was trying to make a decision about her.

She brought her attention back to Bridget.

"Speaking of being a homebody," she said, "I need to get handier with repairs and stuff. There are so many things around the house that need fixing up, but I'm afraid of ruining it if I tackle anything."

"I wish I could help," Bridget said. "But you know I'm no better."

A melodic chime sounded in the café, signaling that someone else had entered. As usual, almost everyone looked to see who the new arrival was. Charlotte followed suit and saw Paul and Tyson coming in.

She had no explanation for the way her heart suddenly sped up.

Tyson had his hands jammed in the pockets of his jeans, and his reddish mop of hair looked like it could use a cut. Beside him, in a black T-shirt that emphasized his broad shoulders and a pair of blue jeans, his uncle looked strong, and like he could handle any situation that life threw his way.

Except Charlotte could still see the shadow of a deep weariness in his eyes. She wanted to know more about him, about what put those shadows in his eyes.

Tyson had spotted her and was sidling up

to their table, looking awestruck to see her. It always entertained Charlotte the way her students acted like they had run into a celebrity—or an alien—if they saw her outside the classroom.

Tyson grinned shyly. "Hi, Ms. Connelly! Did you have breakfast?" he asked.

"I did," Charlotte told him. "The pancakes were delicious."

He nodded as if pondering the secrets of the universe. Paul came over to their table. "Hi," he said glancing at Charlotte, then at Bridget.

"Hi!" Bridget chirped. "And what brings you two handsome gentlemen out this morning?"

"Who's she talking about?" Tyson said in an audible whisper, and Charlotte fought the urge to giggle.

"We've come out for some breakfast, too," Paul answered Bridget. "For a special treat."

"And we forgot to buy eggs," Tyson added.

"I sometimes forget to buy things, too," Charlotte said to Tyson, hoping Paul knew he shouldn't be too hard on himself.

Their gazes met, and his eyes had a glimmer of thanks in them.

"Hey, Paul," Bridget piped up, "I've heard you're good at repairs and things. Char here was just telling me that she could use some help with her house."

Charlotte shot her cousin a warning look.

"Really?" Paul said. "I'd be happy to come over and give you a hand."

"Oh, that's okay, you don't have to," Charlotte said, flustered.

"No, I'd like to," Paul said. "It would mean a lot to me if I could contribute in some way."

Charlotte understood the feeling of wanting to make a contribution.

"Okay, then," she said. "I'd be happy to accept your assistance."

Tyson wandered over to select a coloring book and crayons from the basket Seth kept for the children at the front.

"Did you see those reading sheets I sent home with Tyson?" Charlotte asked. "He's doing quite well, but I think just a bit more practice would really make a difference. I can go over them in more detail with you, if you like?"

For a moment she thought she saw a panicked expression flash across Paul's face, but then it was gone. He gave a tight smile and said, "That's fine, we'll get to them. It's just been a busy week."

Charlotte nodded. "I understand," she said.

She would make sure that she encouraged and supported them both.

"Just know I'm here to help if you need it," she added.

Paul nodded. "I appreciate that," he said. "Got your coloring book?" he called over to Tyson.

"Yup, and crayons, too." The little boy came back to stand beside his uncle.

"Hey, Paul!" Seth hurried over. "Have a seat, and whatever you want, it's on the house. Thanks a lot for looking at the car. We really appreciate it."

"My pleasure."

Paul said the right words, but Charlotte saw from his face that he wasn't comfortable being praised.

"Let's go find a table, Ty," he said to his nephew. "Say goodbye to the ladies."

"Goodbye, ladies," Tyson intoned obediently.

Charlotte grinned. "Enjoy your weekend, Tyson. See you at school on Monday."

Just as they were about to walk away, Paul turned back and asked, "When did you say those community activities were?"

"Wednesday nights," Charlotte said. Paul nodded as he made his way to a table on the other side of the café, where Tyson was sitting.

"What was that all about?" Bridget asked in a hushed tone. "Are you guys friends?"

"His nephew is a student in my class," Charlotte replied, deliberately not answering the question she knew Bridget was really asking.

Especially since there was no other answer to give, was there?

After breakfast at the café, Charlotte went home to do her Saturday chores around the house. As she dusted and swept, her thoughts kept returning to Paul Belvedere. She couldn't escape the nagging feeling that there was something he wasn't telling her. On the other hand, he was trying to connect.

Lord, please be with Paul and Tyson and please help me to help them in the best way I can.

Charlotte picked up the dishcloth and wiped the counter and around the burners of the stove. The motion helped soothe her racing thoughts.

She knew her home would never be as pristinely immaculate as the one she grew up in, but that suited her just fine. She loved the earthy tones, the fact that not everything matched perfectly, her collection of knick-knacks that ranged from lovely to humorous and the fact that her bookshelves bulged from floor to ceiling and still couldn't contain everything she wanted to read.

Her home was her haven, and she was content there. Or at least she had been. Why was it that lately she felt like she wanted to go somewhere where no one knew her? She looked at the computer that sat on her kitchen table and promised herself that she would make time for more missionary-work research later.

She was scrubbing especially hard at a remnant of spaghetti sauce on the stove top when the phone rang, causing her to jump.

"Charlotte, dear, it's Mom." Her mother sounded weary. "How are you? I just wanted to touch base with you."

"I'm fine, Mom," she said. "How was your day? How's your head feeling today? Did you and Dad get to the farmer's market?" Her mother launched into a description of carrots, cucumbers, beets and bartering.

Try as she might to focus, Charlotte's thoughts kept drifting to missionary work. She felt like she was keeping a secret from her parents by not telling them that she was even thinking about it, but she couldn't bring herself to mention it, because it seemed like ever since Anna had died, her parents got through their days by keeping things as much the same as they could. To them, change often signaled something negative.

On Wednesday night, Paul watched Tyson eat his last bite of spaghetti, then immediately leaned in with a washcloth to tackle the orange beard. Tyson yowled and wriggled.

"Quite the performance," Paul observed dryly. The first time Tyson had reacted that way to getting his face cleaned, he had thought he was hurting him and had felt guilty. Now, he realized it was par for the course for a six-year-old and that Ty would be fine in thirty seconds.

Sure enough, his face clean, Tyson asked nonchalantly, "Where are we going again, Uncle Paul?"

"We're going to the church. There are some activities there on Wednesday nights that might be fun."

"What's activities?"

"Games, I think. Maybe some stories and snacks. There's a basketball hoop outside." Paul tried to think of how else to sell the idea to Tyson…or maybe he was trying to sell it to himself. "Your teacher will be there, too, I think."

"Ms. Connelly?"

"Yes, I think so."

"I like stories," Tyson mused, "and games, and maybe basketball."

"See, it will be great!" The enthusiastic tone in Paul's voice sounded slightly false to his own ears. "Put your plate in the sink, please," he told Tyson. "And go brush your teeth. We'll be leaving in five minutes."

Tyson obliged, but then stopped at the bottom of the stairs. "My mom and my dad used to read stories to me. Will you read me stories, Uncle Paul?"

Oh, please, not now...

"What!" Paul feigned exaggerated offense. "What about the continuing saga of 'Ty the Adventure Boy'? You can't tell me that there's a story out there more exciting than that!"

Every night at bedtime, he'd been spinning out tales of a little boy just like Tyson who went on a variety of adventures. So far, Tyson had seemed to love it, but Paul worried that his reprieve was over.

But Tyson didn't say anything else for the moment. He just turned and ran up the rest of the stairs.

He took the few minutes that Tyson would be gone to rinse off their supper dishes. He still wasn't quite used to Tyson's toys and articles of clothing strewn here and there. He preferred his living accommodations to be clean, stark and impersonal. That way nothing felt like home and it was easy to leave when the urge took him.

But you can't do that anymore, he thought. It was different when he had only himself to worry about, but now he had Tyson to consider, and he would for many years to come. It wasn't just that Erica had granted him guardianship of Ty. He knew all too well what it felt like to think no one was on your side, and he was determined that Tyson would never have to feel that way. Thankfully, Ty's teacher felt the same way. He had the primary role in Tyson's life, but the more people the little boy could count on, the better.

Tyson came back down the stairs with his face pink from what looked to be another scrubbing and his hair slicked back and smelling suspiciously like Paul's aftershave.

"Got yourself a little spiffed up there, did you, bud?"

Tyson nodded and beamed, while Paul fervently hoped the walk over would help ease some of the overpowering scent.

The church was about a ten-minute walk from his house, and he knew that there was really no good reason why attending on Sundays couldn't become a regular habit for them. Well, other than the fact that he had lost his desire to attend years ago.

"Will there be kids there that I know?" Tyson asked, and Paul tried to gauge whether there was any apprehension in the question.

"I expect so," he said. "Ms. Connelly said there usually are. You'd like that, wouldn't you?"

Tyson considered and nodded.

"Tyson?"

"Yeah, Uncle Paul?"

"The other kids in your class…they're nice to you, aren't they?"

"Yup. Except…they all have moms and dads." Paul watched his nephew struggle to articulate something that no six-year-old should have to. It was difficult enough for an adult to cope with the impact of such a loss.

"It's okay, Ty," he said softly, giving the boy's shoulder a gentle squeeze. "I totally get it.

"And Ms. Connelly is a good teacher?" he asked, after they continued walking. He thought that she was, but he needed to hear Tyson say it.

"Yeah, she's nice and she's pretty. Do *you* think she's pretty, Uncle Paul?"

He pictured her caring smile and violet

eyes. "Yes, she's pretty." It caught him off guard how much he meant it.

"She's not even married," Tyson added, conversationally. "Hey! Neither are you, Uncle Paul."

Okay, he had to put a rapid stop to wherever Tyson was going with this.

"As long as she's a good teacher and you're happy, that's all that matters to me."

At the front door of the church, Tyson hesitated. "If I don't have fun, we don't have to stay, right?"

"No, we don't," Paul said. "But I hope that you do have fun." He suddenly felt pressured, like he desperately needed this to work out— for both of them. He had to find his place here in town and get along with people as well as he could, even though he always kept his guard up.

He was growing used to the way Tyson's bravado ebbed and flowed. But he wished he knew if that was typical of the age or something specific to Tyson's personality.

There were so many things that he didn't know.

The first person Paul spotted when they stepped inside was Charlotte. Her appearance surprised him. She looked much less rigid dressed in blue jeans and a navy-blue-and-turquoise plaid shirt, with her hair pulled up in a ponytail. She was smiling at someone, and he suddenly wished that he was the recipient of the smile that brought life and beauty to her face. She didn't have the kind of beauty that he had noticed right away. But now he wanted to keep looking.

He found himself drawn in her direction, not even sure what he planned to say to her, only knowing he wanted to be within her reassuring orbit. "There's your teacher," he murmured to Tyson. "Let's go say hello."

They drew closer but just as he was about to get her attention, she called out, "Literacy volunteers for tonight, raise your hands, please!"

Paul stopped and gripped Tyson's hand. Charlotte summoned the volunteers forward and began to give them instructions.

"Char, I'm so happy to hear you're going to apply for overseas missionary work," Paul heard one of the volunteers say. "I think you'll be absolutely perfect for it."

He couldn't hear Charlotte's response, and he was only vaguely aware of Tyson tugging at his hand and saying, "C'mon, Uncle Paul, I wanna say hi to Ms. Connelly."

"She's busy," he answered automatically. "Let's go find something to do."

While his thoughts whirled around in his head, he stopped Tyson's protests by steering him toward a table that held juice and cookies.

Why had Charlotte promised that they would work as a team to help Tyson when her plan was to leave town?

He hoped he hadn't made a huge mistake in coming here…or in trusting her.

Chapter Three

Charlotte tried to focus on setting up tables and chairs in the room where the literacy class was being held, but she was puzzled. She was sure that she had seen Paul and Tyson come in and start heading in her direction, but by the time she was finished instructing the volunteers, they were nowhere to be seen.

Well, she would try to catch up with them later. They had a full house tonight. She noticed that the tired, rather bedraggled-looking woman and her young son, whom Bridget had asked about at Seth's, were there again. They stayed close to the snack table, and she pondered approaching them to see if they wanted to join in any of the activities. But the last time she had done so, the woman had responded in a prickly manner that had set Charlotte back on her heels. Still, she believed that the church was open to all and guessed that they just wanted a place to be without being bombarded with questions.

The little boy—if she remembered correctly, his name was Michael Cannon—had joined the other children for stories and games last week, but he hadn't interacted much, and his mother had been anxious to leave as soon as the evening was over.

Charlotte reminded herself to ask around to see if anyone knew more about them, and to pray for them.

"Charlotte, can you give me a hand setting out the materials?"

She snapped herself out of her musings to see Stephanie Winslow, a pretty young pharmacy assistant who worked at Dudley's, holding an armful of books, sheets of paper and a box of pencils.

"Sorry, Steph, be right there." She hurried over to relieve Stephanie of some of her load.

As the two women got things organized, other volunteers came through the door— Seth and Rena were there, Dudley and his wife, and a couple of teenage boys from youth group.

"Good of you to come out." Charlotte smiled at them.

The literacy volunteer group worked mainly

with immigrants who were learning English. Usually Charlotte loved interacting with the students. She loved their eagerness and willingness to learn and seeing the way their eyes would light up with pride and understanding when they grasped something. But, for some reason, on this particular night she couldn't concentrate.

Her thoughts kept returning to Paul and Tyson. She wondered where they had gone—if they had even stayed—and what activities they had chosen. She tried telling herself that she was only concerned for Tyson, but she had to admit that she was also worried about his handsome uncle. She wondered what had prompted him to come tonight when she had been so sure that he wouldn't.

But perhaps the biggest question was why did it matter to her so much? Was she already getting too involved, not only in her concern for Tyson but also by accepting Paul's offer of help around her house? She was Tyson's teacher and committed to helping him, but she didn't want to risk too strong a connection knowing full well that she could be gone by the end of June.

But asking herself those questions didn't stop her from wanting to track them down.

"Would you mind getting things started?"

she asked Stephanie. "I have something I have to check on."

Stephanie quirked a curious eyebrow at her but nodded.

"Thanks. I promise I won't be long."

Charlotte stepped out into the main fellowship room and looked around. She spotted Tyson by the snack table, where he was exchanging wary glances with Michael. The latter boy's mother was nowhere in sight, although Paul lingered close by, keeping a watchful eye on both boys.

"Where's your mom, Michael?" Charlotte asked. He looked surly and older than his years.

"Went to read in the library. She said she needed quiet time."

"There are stories and games for you boys, if you like," Charlotte said. She glanced at Paul, who looked ready to pounce.

"If that's okay with you," she said to him. "Eugenie, from Seth's café, is supervising the kids tonight. I promise she's very good with them."

"Would you like to go, Ty?" Paul asked.

"I guess…" the little boy said.

Tyson looked uneasily at Michael, who shifted from one foot to the other and said, "I guess I'll just go sit with my mom. I know

I have to be quiet," he said, answering a question that hadn't been asked.

As soon as Michael was gone, Tyson said with more conviction, "I want to go."

"I'll show you where the room is." Charlotte offered him her hand, which he grasped onto.

Paul followed closely behind them. "What's with that kid? Michael?" he asked in a low tone so Tyson couldn't hear him.

"I'm not sure," Charlotte admitted. "They don't live in Green Valley, and he's not at my school. I get the feeling they haven't had an easy time of it."

"Probably not," Paul said. "I hope things work out for them, whatever the issue is, but I have to say I'm glad he's not in your class."

"Why is that?" Charlotte asked.

"Let's just say, I know the type."

She turned a questioning face to him, but his was unreadable.

Charlotte handed off Tyson to Eugenie. He soon had a book in one hand, a cookie in the other and a nose-crinkling grin on his face.

"Have fun, sport," Paul said to Tyson. "I'll be right out here at…?"

"At eight o'clock," Charlotte said. "Eugenie will tell you when it's time to go."

She knew she needed to get back to her

group, but she wondered what Paul planned to do for the remainder of the evening.

"Would you like to join our group?" she asked him. "The more the merrier."

As she extended what was meant to be just a friendly invitation, she suddenly realized how much she wanted him to say yes.

For one mindless moment, Paul felt like he'd follow the teacher and her bright smile wherever she was going. But then it struck him that, of course, she meant that he could come along and help teach. He felt his mouth quirk into an unamused smile. It didn't help either that he still carried his discomfort from what he had overheard earlier.

"When I came to see you about Tyson," he began.

"Yes?" Charlotte encouraged.

"You said that it was important for us to work as a team."

"Which is true." She tilted her head and gave him a puzzled smile.

"So, why didn't you happen to mention that you're planning to go away?" In answer to her startled face, he added, "I overheard one of the volunteers."

"I'm only thinking about going," Charlotte confirmed. She straightened her shoulders and met his gaze. "I haven't made a final decision yet, but even if I do end up going, it won't be until after the school year has ended. I meant what I said, Paul. I have no intentions of leaving while Tyson is still in my class."

Paul studied her. It all sounded good, but only time would tell if her actions matched her words. He had been hurt and disappointed by too many people in the past. He wished her eyes weren't quite so big and expressive and made an effort to gentle his tone. "I guess we'll see how it goes, then."

Her shoulders relaxed a bit. "Okay, thank you. Would you like to join us?" She extended the invitation again.

"No, thanks," Paul said. "I'm more of a physical-activity type."

"There's the basketball hoop outside," Charlotte reminded him. "You could join your fellow jocks."

Your fellow jocks... A memory slammed into him involving some grade eight boys from the basketball team.

It took every ounce of self-control he had to say lightly, "I guess I meant I'm more of a fix-it kind of guy. I don't suppose you have any light bulbs that need changing, or a furnace filter that's overdue for a swap?"

Charlotte studied him with a puzzled look

on her face. "You want to spend your time here fixing things?"

"Or whatever needs doing."

"I thought you'd come here to get to know people better?" she asked.

She was right, of course, and he would do whatever it took, as long as Tyson was safe and happy here. He just wouldn't go shoot hoops with a group of men who would bring back memories of how the jocks in school had treated him.

"I do want that," Paul said. "But I think you can get to know people working on projects together. Plus, these older buildings usually have a lot of neglected areas because no one has the time or inclination to get to them— kind of like you and your house," he couldn't resist adding and grinned to see how flustered the sometimes prim schoolteacher could look.

"Yeah, yeah," she said, waving her hand. Then she said, "I just thought of something— wait right here."

Paul stood there, wondering what she had in mind. Charlotte returned a few minutes later, looking pleased with herself.

"We have more than our quota of volunteers tonight," she said, "so I'm getting Stephanie to take over for me and I'm going to take you on a tour of the place and introduce you to a couple of gentlemen who have been keeping a long-running list of the things that never get done."

Again, he had conflicted feelings about Charlotte. She appeared to be so engaged in helping him and Tyson, which he supposed went along with her role as a teacher and a volunteer. But he couldn't allow himself or Tyson to get too attached to her. The end of the school year would come before they knew it, and it was very likely she would be gone.

Besides, what reason would he possibly have to get attached to her besides wanting what was best for Tyson?

Soon, he found himself engaged in conversation with Ralph Meyer, a retired police officer, and Joe Rockaberry, who had owned the grocery store in town for years before selling it to his son-in-law. They both had an avid interest in keeping things shipshape at the church. It was clear that their white hair and aging bodies had no impact on the sharpness of their minds or the validity of their ideas.

As they chatted about what Paul could help with, a quietly optimistic voice in the back of his mind said, *I can do this. This is all going to work out.* He caught Charlotte's eye then, and was warmed by the encouraging nod that she gave him. But again he reminded himself not to count on her encouragement too much. His entire life had taught him that he couldn't really count on anyone. Ever.

"We should sit somewhere," Joe suggested. "Put some kind of plan together."

The remainder of the time went by rapidly, as the three men sat in one of the meeting rooms and decided what projects would take priority. Soon Paul found himself back at the classroom door, waiting for Tyson to come out. He tried not to, but he caught himself watching for a glimpse of Charlotte's blue plaid shirt and the bounce of her ponytail.

Just then, Tyson came out of the room, chattering the instant he saw his uncle.

"We had so many stories, Uncle Paul! Did you know David slewed Goliath even though he was *way* smaller and did you know that Max is my new friend and that she's a girl, not a boy, even though her name is Max, and I want to come back next week, okay, can we?"

When he finally stopped to take a breath, Paul smiled. "I'm glad you enjoyed yourself so much. Yes, we can come back."

Tyson jumped around excitedly. "Hey, Max," he said to the little girl who had come to stand beside him, "I get to come back next week."

Max was tiny and blonde, wore pink overalls and had pink ribbons on her pigtails, so Paul was amused at how deep and froggy her voice was. "That's great, Ty!"

Just then, he spotted Charlotte across the room. She was smiling at a woman and holding a wriggling child in her arms while the woman put her coat on.

Then he saw the library door open and a bedraggled woman emerged, looking like she'd just awoken from a nap. She held Michael's hand but seemed detached from him.

He saw Michael look over at Tyson and frown. A shot of apprehension went through Paul, but Tyson was engrossed in making silly faces with Max and hadn't noticed.

He reassured himself that the boy wasn't in Tyson's class. The evening at church had gone better than he'd expected, and he didn't want anything to spoil it.

Charlotte's peal of laughter bounced across the room. Paul looked over to see that she was giggling at the antics of a toddler. He noticed other eyes were on her, too. Michael's mother's frown mimicked her son's.

Charlotte had said she didn't know them. So why was the woman looking at Charlotte like she was angry at her about something?

Charlotte came over to Paul and Tyson

and said, "I'm really glad you came tonight. I hope you had fun."

"I sure did," Tyson said.

"It was great," Paul said. "I'm sure we'll be back. Thanks for introducing me to Ralph and Joe. They're great guys."

"You're welcome," Charlotte said, her eyes shining with pleasure. "See you soon."

Paul found himself thinking that was something he hoped would happen. He definitely wanted to see Charlotte again soon.

Chapter Four

On her way home from school on Thursday, Charlotte popped into the pharmacy to pick up one of her favorite women's magazines to read with her evening tea, and also to ask Stephanie how the rest of the night had gone with the literacy volunteer group.

"I felt bad about leaving you guys," she said. "But it was Paul and Tyson's first time there, and I wanted to make sure that they felt welcome."

Stephanie looked over the rim of her glasses at Charlotte. "I'm sure you did," she teased.

"Oh, stop it," Charlotte protested in a light tone. Because she was in her mid-twenties and not married, it went with the territory to be teased about every eligible man that came along. But still, she wished others would understand that she had no idea when she would seriously consider marriage. She was still trying to decide her life, let alone trying to incorporate a relationship into the equation, even with someone as undeniably attractive as Paul.

"All joking aside," Stephanie said, "the group was great. We missed you, of course, but we got a lot done. You know, it's not just reading that they need help with, it's a whole bunch of practical things, like how to take public transportation, how to open up a bank account, that kind of thing."

"I know." Charlotte nodded. "We really have to make sure that we remember that many of them are starting a whole new life here and the things we take for granted are things that are totally new to them." She added, "I noticed that boy Michael and his mother were there again, too. Has anyone had a chance to find out more about them?"

Stephanie shook her head. "I think a few people tried, but they don't make themselves very approachable. I have the feeling that the church isn't so much a place they want to be as a place they're using to get *away* from something, if that makes any sense."

Or from someone? Charlotte found herself wondering. But before they could explore the subject any further, an older gentleman stepped into the pharmacy and Stephanie excused herself to assist him.

Once she was home, Charlotte sliced up some vegetables into the salad she was making for supper. As she twisted open the cap on a bottle of salad dressing, she thought about the previous evening and the time she had spent with Paul Belvedere to welcome him to the church community. She prayed that it had been a good experience for him. She noticed that Tyson had been more outgoing in class today. Of course, Charlotte thought with amusement, he looked more than happy to let Max Hansen lead the way.

When Charlotte slid the silverware drawer open to get a fork, the drawer stuck as it always did. She frowned as she wiggled it gently to and fro. Finally the drawer opened, but instead of feeling satisfied, she sighed and mentally added it to the seemingly endless list of things in the house that needed fixing. Besides the sticky drawer, she needed more shelf space, the walls needed paint touch-ups, the leg on one of the kitchen chairs was wobbly and the light in the storage room remained out because she was intimidated by the light fixture cover.

She thought of Paul's offer to come over

and help, and as she pictured his large presence in her kitchen, it did funny things to her pulse again. She wondered how she would possibly muster the courage to go overseas if she was thwarted by a few repairs. She didn't want to need Paul's help, but maybe if he could give her a few pointers, she could handle the rest. She wanted to be a strong, independent woman who could take care of herself and who had something to give back to the world.

And, Lord, I want to stop feeling terrible about Anna every single day of my life.

Then she did what she always did when guilt and regret threatened to consume her: she brought herself back into the present by being practical. She grabbed a pen and paper and started to make a list of things she would need to do if she was truly going to consider the missionary work. At least that way she could feel one step closer to her goal.

When she began writing her list, her phone rang. When Charlotte saw her parents' number come up, she briefly considered letting it go to voice mail, but then thought better of it.

"Hi, Mom," she said.

"Actually, it's Dad."

"Dad? Is everything all right?" Charlotte asked. Her father rarely called her.

"Yes," he continued. "I just needed to let you know that I'm worried about your mother. Her health doesn't appear to be improving and the doctors aren't able to give us any solid answers. I'm actually afraid she might be getting worse. But you know your mother—you can't get her to take a break from anything."

Charlotte was concerned about her mother, too, but the timing of the phone call discouraged her from believing she'd ever get a chance to do the missionary work. But maybe she wasn't meant to go and her role was to be there for her parents, because what had happened to Anna was her fault. And now, to add to that, she found it hard to shake the uneasy feeling she got knowing that Paul had doubted her good intentions when he'd heard she was thinking of going away.

But she had told God she was sorry. She had told Him so many times she had lost count.

Dear Lord, can't I please be allowed to have a fulfilling life of my own?

"Charlotte? Are you still there?" She could hear the strain in her father's voice. He didn't like talking on the phone, so she knew he must be very worried to have called her.

"I can talk to Mom," she said. "Try to get her to slow down, and we'll definitely keep on the doctors to look for what's causing her severe headaches. But, like you said, you know how she is."

"Thanks, honey. I appreciate you trying," her father said. "We'll see you tomorrow for supper."

"Yes, see you tomorrow night."

After they hung up, Charlotte started adding more items to her list. But unspoken questions buzzed around in her head and she put the pen down. She decided that she would go for a walk to try to clear her head instead.

And, Lord, she continued her prayer, *am I ever going to feel Your forgiveness?*

Because, despite what the Bible said, she didn't feel forgiven for not protecting Anna, not in the slightest.

On Friday morning, Paul was in a good mood—mostly because Tyson was in such a fine one. It was remarkable how quickly his life had been become impacted by the little boy—this adorable legacy of his sister.

"Max knows everything," Tyson said as he shoved cereal into his mouth. "She's going to show me at recess how to tie knots like they tie them for ships."

"A good skill for anyone to have," Paul said. Speaking of skills, he wondered if Charlotte would take him up on his offer to help fix up her house. He had to admit he was curious to see what kind of home she had and how it reflected her personality.

"That's what I thought, too," Tyson agreed, with enthusiasm. "Uncle Paul, can you believe that Max and I were in the same class and we didn't even notice each other and now we're best friends?"

"That's something for sure."

"Maybe you and Ms. Connelly could be best friends or get married or something." Tyson nodded as if something obvious had been decided and set his spoon down.

"We'll stick with friends for now, okay, sport? Take your dishes to the sink and go brush your teeth. We're leaving in five minutes."

A picture of Charlotte's laughing face came into his mind. That made him smile.

After Paul had dropped Tyson off at school, he was relieved to get to work and let the busyness of the day take over and not give him time to think about other things. Although he fervently hoped that Mrs. Meissner wouldn't be one of his customers today.

Constantly hiding his illiteracy was exhausting. It had always made him acutely aware of what people did and didn't pay attention to. No one ever questioned him, for example, in a restaurant if he just pretended to glance at a menu and said, "That sounds good. I'll have the same." These days no one even blinked if you hadn't read a particular book or news article, since it was so quick and easy to keep up with current events by other means.

But all of that didn't make him feel any better about it. He was tired of hiding, but every time he thought of doing something about it, he was frozen with fear.

Once again, he wondered how it would feel to share his secret with Charlotte.

Just before noon there was a lull at the garage, and Paul settled himself on a stool in the back to eat the ham and cheese sandwich he'd hastily made that morning.

When Harold came into the back to find him, he braced himself for the worst. But all Harold said was, "It was great to see you at church on Wednesday night. That's the kind of thing that people here in town really appreciate."

"Tyson and I enjoyed ourselves," Paul replied.

"Carry on, then," Harold said cheerfully. "I'm heading out for a bit. I shouldn't be gone too long."

A few minutes after he left, the door chimed again, and Paul went to the front to see who had come in. He was caught off guard at how glad he felt to see that it was Charlotte.

She was back in teacher mode, wearing a gray jacket, white blouse and gray pants, and she had her hair smoothed back into a tidy bun. He thought about how she'd looked on Wednesday night with her jeans, and her soft, loose hair and her ready laugh.

"It's like there are two different versions of you."

Had he really just said that out loud?

For a second, Charlotte gave him an odd look.

"I...ah—" he fumbled for the right thing to say. "I mean, your hairstyles..."

"Oh..." Charlotte's hand reflexively went up to the bun, and she smiled uncertainly.

"You look great both ways," Paul said. "I mean..."

She also smelled good, the light scent of her soap reaching him, and he cleared his throat, feeling awkward.

Then Charlotte laughed and broke the moment. "It's okay," she said. "I think I know what you mean. I have to dress more professionally for work but, between you and me, I'd live in my jeans if I could."

Changing the subject, Paul asked, "So, what can I do for you?"

"I, ah… I want to take you up on your offer. I mean, could you come over sometime and look at the things that need doing around my place?"

"I'd be happy to," Paul said, grinning. "How about Saturday morning after breakfast?"

Charlotte nodded, looking like she had accomplished something big just by asking. "That would be great," she said. "I really appreciate it."

"No problem. I'm glad you asked." He surprised himself with how much he meant it.

It didn't mean he was getting involved with her, he was quick to remind himself. She was helping him with Tyson, and he was helping her in return. A fair exchange.

"Did Ty have a good morning?" he asked, returning to a subject that was safe for both of them.

"Yes, he had a great morning. We talked about different kinds of pets this morning. What makes a good one and what doesn't. I apologize in advance, because I think you might be hit with the 'Can I have a dog?' question any day now."

He chuckled. "I appreciate the heads-up."

The door chime signaled another arrival to the shop.

"Charlotte? I thought I saw you in here!" Charlotte's cousin Bridget poked her head into the office. "I'm just on a break and was on my way to grab a sandwich at Seth's."

"Bridget is an assistant at the vet clinic," Charlotte explained.

"Hi, Bridget," Paul said, trying not to be too obvious in his disappointment that his conversation with Charlotte had been interrupted. "Good to see you again," he added politely.

"Nice to see you, too," Bridget answered. She linked her arm through Charlotte's. "Walk over with me, Char?"

"In a moment," Charlotte said. Paul noticed that she didn't seem in a hurry for their conversation to end.

"By the way, have you talked to your parents about mission work?" Bridget asked. "Just think, Char, this time next year you could be halfway across the world!"

"Yes, imagine that," Paul said coolly. "Well, I won't keep you ladies any longer, then," he added. "Enjoy the rest of your lunch break."

"Will you still be coming over to help out?" Charlotte asked hesitantly.

"Yes, I promise I'll be there," Paul said.

He could only hope that she took her own promises as seriously.

Chapter Five

What exactly was the appropriate thing to wear when a handsome bachelor was coming over to teach her about home improvements?

Charlotte's nervous hands moved her clothes back and forth in her closet. She knew it was just a poor attempt to ignore the real question: Did Paul Belvedere like her or not? One moment he acted like he did, and the next it seemed like he couldn't wait for her to leave, like when Bridget had come into Harold's during their conversation at lunch yesterday. She told herself that it wasn't so much that she wanted him to like her; she just needed him to trust that she was a good teacher for Tyson and had their best interests at heart.

Frustrated, she yanked a purple shirt off a hanger and found an old pair of jeans on the top shelf of her closet. She dressed quickly, put on enough makeup to look presentable but not like she was trying too hard, and checked to see that the coffee was on.

She had just finished putting her hair into a braid when there was a knock at the door. She took a deep breath and opened it to see Paul standing on her doorstep, holding a large toolbox. His masculine good looks made her foolishly wish that she had taken more time with her appearance. She pushed the thought aside. This wasn't about them making a romantic connection. This was about learning practical skills that would help her to feel more independent. That's what she wanted, after all—independence, not forming ties that were bound to break.

"Am I too early?" Paul asked, and Charlotte realized that she'd let him just stand there on the doorstep.

"Not at all," she said hurriedly. "Please come in. Where's Tyson, by the way?"

"He's over at Max's."

As he stepped into the entryway, she tried to see her house through his eyes. She knew she was a tidy but not immaculate housekeeper, and that the decor reflected her personality rather than the latest trends.

"Come into the kitchen," Charlotte said. "That's probably the best place to start."

Paul set the toolbox on the kitchen table and looked around. "I like your place," he said. "It's very you."

She was inordinately pleased, but then something in Paul's eyes shut down again. "I don't mean that I really know you," he said. "Just that I noticed there's some variety in how you've fixed up the place, like you have different ways that you dress and wear your hair."

Feeling self-conscious, Charlotte tugged on her braid. "I knew what you meant," she hurried to say. "I don't like everything matchy-matchy," she added, thinking of her mother's house, where the curtains matched the sofa and the wallpaper.

Silence hovered between them.

Paul cleared his throat. "So…what do you want to show me first?" he asked.

"Maybe we could start by changing the light bulb in the storage room," Charlotte suggested.

With Paul coaching and encouraging, she climbed up on the step ladder and managed to remove the cover off the light fixture. Paul was good at explaining things without making her feel like she had six extra arms, none of which had any coordination at all. "I did it!" she said, back on the ground and feeling pleased with herself.

"You sure did," Paul praised her. "Next I'll show you how to hammer a nail without hitting your thumb."

They moved on to the next task, and after they'd successfully hung all of Charlotte's pictures, Paul said, "I've got to take you shopping for your own tool kit. There are things that no house should be without."

"Or you could just make me a list," Charlotte suggested. "I'd hate to take up more of your time."

"I don't mind," Paul said tersely. "But I should probably leave soon, to pick up Ty."

"Can you stay just a little while longer?" Charlotte asked. "I made coffee. I'd like to show you some hospitality to thank you for helping me."

"That's very kind of you," Paul said, as he sat down at the kitchen table and accepted a mug of coffee.

"I think I might have some leftover Saskatoon berry muffins from Seth's, if you like," Charlotte offered.

Paul shook his head. "I had a big breakfast."

As he sipped his coffee, Charlotte noticed

that his eyes had taken on their weary look again, and once more she felt that Paul had concerns above and beyond being Tyson's guardian.

She couldn't resist making another attempt to reach him, even if that meant risking another rejection. "Paul, is there anything else you'd like to talk about? I mean it, anything at all. You know, helping a student involves more than just dealing with the student. I care about what's happening in the families, too, because that can impact the student."

Paul's large hand curved around the cup, and he stared down at the coffee inside.

"It's good of you to care, Charlotte," he said with an expression that she couldn't read.

"I know moving here has been a big adjustment for you," she continued, "You're probably not used to kids, and you're still grieving your sister…"

He raised his eyes and gave her a long, searching look. She almost held her breath, thinking for a moment that he was about to open up. But then his eyes dropped again and he said, "I appreciate your concern, I honestly do. But Ty and I…we'll muddle along. I just want you to keep making sure he's doing all right in school, okay?"

"Of course," Charlotte nodded, trying not

to feel disappointed that she hadn't gotten further with him, but she couldn't force him to say anything he didn't want to. Besides, maybe it was only her imagination that there was anything else to discuss.

Still, something needled her...

"I'm glad I got that light bulb changed and hung those pictures," she said, noticing how Paul relaxed once she'd changed the subject. "Thank you again."

"You're welcome," Paul said. "We'll find a time to pick out some basic tools that will be handy for you to have around and I can come over again, maybe next Saturday? You'd mentioned painting, too. I expect you'll want to pick out colors, but let me know when you want to get that done, too."

Charlotte laughed nervously. "I was thinking of hiring a professional for that."

Paul shook his head. "You don't want to spend that kind of money. Trust me, you can do it yourself for half the cost. Besides, you might even enjoy it."

He smiled at her, a relaxed, open smile, and she had to stand up quickly to take their coffee cups to the sink before he saw the effect he had on her.

Then Paul stood up. "I really have to go. I'm sure I'll see you soon."

"Yes, we're bound to run into each other," she said, smiling at him.

Paul reached forward and gave her braid a gentle tug.

"I like this look on you," he said. Charlotte blushed profusely as she walked him out.

After he left, Charlotte felt like a daydreaming schoolgirl. Then her phone rang and she grabbed it up, glad of the distraction.

"Hi, Bridge," she answered.

"You sure had Anna on your mind at supper last night," Bridget said, not wasting any time getting to the point. "But you know it's upsetting for everyone when you talk about what happened."

Daydreams of a handsome handyman bachelor quickly disappeared.

A million answers, none of them adequate, rushed through Charlotte's mind. Finally she said, "I'm tired of never talking about her, and I think she deserves to be remembered."

"I'm just concerned that you keep tormenting yourself with it, Char."

Then the fight went out of Charlotte as suddenly as it had arrived and she felt as deflated as a damaged tire on the side of the road. She didn't want to upset her family, even if it meant bottling up her own feelings. So she changed the subject to something she knew would interest her cousin.

"I decided you were right about Paul."

"Oh? Why do you say that?"

"I asked him to come over and help me with some fix-it projects around the house. We got a lot done. So thank you for the suggestion."

She didn't tell Bridget about the questions that still troubled her. What good would that have done?

"Do we have a grocery list?" Tyson asked Paul later on that afternoon. "My mom's grocery list was always on the fridge with a magnet that was a bumblebee."

Paul tensed up a little. When Tyson mentioned his parents, he still never knew if it was going to be just a passing remark or a spiral downward into a session of grief and the impossible demand that his parents be returned to him.

But this time, Tyson just looked curious, and Paul breathed a sigh of relief. For the moment, he was free to think about the morning he'd spent helping Charlotte. She was a quick learner and was more adept at things than she gave herself credit for. He'd wanted to tell her so, but he was torn between being drawn to her and keeping up his walls. Especially since she was going to leave town soon. He tried to tell himself that he was only concerned for Tyson's sake, but it was getting harder and harder to do that.

"Uncle Paul?" Tyson repeated. "Do we have a list?"

"It's all up here," Paul tapped the side of his head with one finger and pulled a funny face that made Tyson laugh. He relied on his memory, compensating for not being able to read.

"Saturday we call Grandpa Glen and Grandma Pat, right?" Tyson's question steered his thoughts away from Charlotte.

"Yes, that's right." He believed it was good for Tyson to connect to whatever family he had left, even if he was never sure how much the phone calls meant to his parents.

They had retired to Victoria, British Columbia, and during their Saturday evening phone visits, they chatted enthusiastically about life in their senior living complex, which, as far as Paul could tell, provided plenty of friends, lots of activities and a variety of delicious meals. He knew that both of his parents had worked very hard to provide for their family throughout the years, so he tried not to begrudge them a well-earned early retirement. But it reminded him of the way they had always been such a self-contained unit—working long hours to provide for his and his sister's physical needs but letting the details of their lives slip through the cracks. Details from the small, like Erica and her best friend having a brief fight, to large ones... Paul closed his eyes briefly.

That was then. This is now. I'm not that boy anymore.

He knew they must have grieved Erica's loss greatly. But they'd handled the funeral and other details and carried on with their lives in such a pragmatic way it was almost impossible to tell exactly how they felt about losing their only daughter.

Paul vowed again that Tyson would never have to wonder how Paul felt about him.

At the grocery store, Paul was surprised when he spotted Charlotte in the hardware aisle. She held two packages of nails in her hands and frowned at both of them. Her frown made him want to grin from ear to ear. She was wearing blue jeans, a pair that looked newer than the ones she'd worn that morning, and a mint-green sweater. But she had her hair pulled back, teacher style—a hybrid of the two Charlottes.

He suddenly realized that she was trying to pick out nails on her own, even though he'd told her he was willing to help. He wondered what that meant.

Tyson caught sight of her, too, and called out, "Ms. Connelly!" as he careened toward her. "Hey it's me, Tyson!"

"It is you!" Charlotte said to Tyson, matching his enthusiasm. She ruffled his already unruly hair. "It's great to see you. I see you're helping your uncle get the grocery shopping done." She turned her gaze to Paul. "I guess we're seeing each other again even sooner than we thought."

He nodded, trying to decide if she was embarrassed or if he was only imagining it.

"Uncle Paul doesn't use a list," Tyson said, with an eye roll that made his feelings clear on the matter.

"His memory must be better than mine," Charlotte said. "I'd be lost without one."

Paul didn't want any more conversation about memory or lists, so he changed the subject. "You look like you could use some help there," he said, indicating the nails. "Though I thought I'd made it clear that I'd help you with that." He looked pointedly at her.

"I know," Charlotte said with an shy smile that tugged as his heart. "But I feel silly asking. I should be able to do these things on my own."

"We all need help with one thing or another, don't we?" Paul said. "Here, let's have a look. No one is born knowing this stuff."

As soon as he said it, an idea flashed into his head. "You know how you're helping the newcomers with their reading and communication?" he said, his words tumbling out rapidly. "Well, there could be other skills they could learn that I could teach them, like basic car maintenance and easy home repairs. Things that everyone could make use of. You could come, too, though of course I'm still willing to help you on a personal level if you…"

He stopped talking. He probably sounded like a blathering idiot.

Charlotte laughed.

"I didn't mean…" Paul said.

"No, I know what you mean. It's okay."

"Ms. Connelly, your cheeks are red," Tyson said.

"Ah, yes… I think it's a bit warm in here." She smiled. "I think it sounds like a really good idea," Charlotte said, trying to recover her composure. "Let's talk more about it on Wednesday night."

"Sounds good," Paul said. "And, by the way, you might as well get both kinds of nails."

"When in doubt, buy more than you need?" Charlotte asked in a teasing tone.

"Exactly," he said. "See, you're learning already."

They parted ways, and Paul was glad that Tyson occupied himself by dashing ahead in the aisles and grabbing what was needed. At least it provided some respite from the constant chatter about his teacher.

"I like Ms. Connelly," he said blissfully. "She shops for groceries like we do, right, Uncle Paul? Do you like her, Uncle Paul?"

"She's a nice woman," Paul answered carefully. "I'm glad you're happy she's your teacher."

He wondered how involved he should really be getting with Charlotte or with the community in general. The problem with getting too close to people was that they could hurt you or find out things about you that you didn't want them to know. He had not been part of a church community for years, and he hoped that people wouldn't think that helping out meant he was interested in letting God in again. Still, for Tyson's sake, he felt he had to give back to the community he was now living in. And maybe helping others would help him to feel less like an outsider.

But he'd do whatever it took to guard his

heart against a certain violet-eyed teacher who was making her way closer him—and to the things he didn't want anyone to know about.

Chapter Six

In the teacher's lounge on Monday, Charlotte bit into her ham and cheese sandwich and listened to Rena sing Paul Belvedere's praises.

"Our car is running perfectly, thanks to him. He's really good at what he does and seems like a great guy."

Charlotte was surprised at the tug of emotion she felt, like she wanted her friends to approve of Paul. And she kept thinking about the way he had helped and encouraged her on Saturday morning, and the sheer pleasure that had skittered through her when she saw him again at the grocery store.

Proceed with caution, she told herself, echoing the lesson she had taught the children that morning about traffic lights as another way to help them recognize colors. She asked God to help her determine the best way to do that.

Now Rena was looking at her with a mischievous light of interest in her brown eyes, so she steered the conversation in a safer direction.

"I actually ran into Paul and Tyson at the grocery store on Saturday afternoon, and we touched on the idea of him teaching basic car and home maintenance skills to the literacy group participants."

"That sounds like a great idea," Rena said.

"I think so, too," Charlotte agreed.

"So, that means you'll probably have to spend more time together?" Rena asked with feigned innocence.

"He's one of my students' uncles," Charlotte said, avoiding her friend's teasing question. "I'm bound to interact with him on a regular basis."

Rena gave her a look that said she wasn't buying it. She was relieved to be rescued from more scrutiny when Rena had to leave because there were a couple of things she needed to get done before the lunch break was over.

When her friend was gone, she immediately felt the weight of silence asking its own questions. Why was she letting her feelings about Paul distract her from her own goals? She pulled the application for missionary work out of her purse and looked it over for what felt like the hundredth time.

Enough of this nonsense, she told herself. She needed to fill out this form and submit it, and she needed to tell her parents about her plans as soon as possible. She was the only child her parents had left and they counted on seeing her on a regular basis, so it was only fair that she give them time to get used to the idea.

The bell rang, signaling that lunchtime was over. Charlotte folded up the application and put it back in her purse. She resolved that she would tell her parents that evening.

Please help me find the words, Lord, and please help them to understand why I need to do this and how important it is to me to pursue a dream.

"Tyson and I really enjoyed the activities at the church last Wednesday night," Paul said to Harold, wanting him to know that he cared about the Green Valley community and that he was getting involved.

They were taking advantage of a lull on Monday to better organize some of the shelves in the shop. Doing so made Paul think about Charlotte and the projects he was helping her with. If he was being honest with himself, thoughts of her were becoming more and more frequent. There was just something about her that made him feel good, comfortable…even safe. Thinking about their most recent conversation at the grocery store the other day reminded him that he wanted to share his idea about teaching basic skills with Harold.

"I wanted to tell you about an idea I had for Wednesdays—something I know I'd be good at."

Harold made a quick note on the pad he carried, then set it aside to give Paul his full attention. He listened carefully as Paul told him what he and Charlotte had discussed on Saturday.

"I think it's a good idea," he said. "You'll have to run it by the organizing committee, but I can't see them saying no to it. And I have to say it's a shame one of us didn't think of it sooner. You probably know that Charlotte Connelly runs the literacy group, so I expect you'll want to get her on board and the two of you will work something out."

"I've already touched base with her about it," Paul said. "In fact, she was the first person I discussed it with, and she's all for it."

Harold gave a satisfied nod. "Well, there you go."

Paul was unable to resist asking, "So…have you known Charlotte for a long time?"

"I've known her practically her whole life," Harold said. "She's a lovely girl, a good person."

The genuine affection on Harold's face as he spoke made his boss, who could sometimes be rough around the edges, look like a real softy. He was curious to hear more.

"Is she a good teacher, too?" he probed, not wanting it to seem like he was probing.

"Oh, I would think so. The kids all seem to love her, and the parents, too. She comes from a good family, of course. I tell you, the way they carried on after…"

The bell rang as a customer entered the shop.

"Duty calls!" Harold gave a sharp salute. "I'll get that." He headed to the front of the shop, leaving Paul to wonder what Harold had been about to say.

Harold's praise of Charlotte should have reassured him, but instead he felt more agitated. He didn't need any more reasons to feel attached—and attracted—to her than he already did.

When Harold returned a few moments

later, he was in full business mode again. "It's getting busy out there. We'll have to get back to this later. It was good to see you and the little guy at church on Wednesday. Maybe you'll think about Sunday, too? There's a terrific Sunday school program that I know Tyson would love."

He said it in an amiable way, but still, Paul felt pressure weighing down on him. He knew that church had been a regular part of Tyson's life and that Erica had probably assumed that Paul would continue on with his spiritual upbringing when she named him as guardian.

It was yet another way that he was falling short.

He forced himself to smile at Harold. "I'll think about it."

It wasn't a lie, because he always thought about it, whether he wanted to or not. He just didn't intend to do anything about it. There was almost nothing that he wouldn't do for Tyson, but this was one barrier he just couldn't push himself past.

On Monday evening, Charlotte sat quietly in her favorite comfy chair and tried to gather her thoughts. She had just told her parents about her plans to do missionary work abroad.

On the one hand, her parents had told her that they understood it was important and valuable work she wanted to do. But there had been apprehension and worry in her mother's voice. "I'm just afraid that something will happen to you, Charlotte."

Her father had lingered on the phone after her mother had gone to lie down with a headache. "With things still being so up in the air with your mother's health, we really need you here, Charlotte."

She tried to tell them that she wouldn't be going away until June of the following year at the earliest, but it didn't appease them.

Now she tried to pray that she would make the right decision, but God wasn't giving her any clear answers. She felt like she had no choice but to follow her heart. Except now she didn't even know what her heart was telling her. At first it had seemed crystal clear that she was meant to go away, but lately she'd been feeling like there were reasons—and people—to stay for.

But if she did that, she would be breaking the promise she had made to herself to stop basing her decisions around other people's expectations.

After what felt like a long time, she stood up and took the application out of her purse.

She spread it out on the kitchen table and ran her hand over it once or twice. Then sat down and began to fill it out.

"Did you eat anything today that you haven't had before?" Paul asked Tyson, trying to keep the urgency out of his voice.

"Just the fruit you cutted up for my bedtime snack," Tyson said, sniffling. Below his tear-filled and swollen eyes, his cheeks were blotchy with red patches.

Paul had sliced up a pineapple for Tyson's bedtime snack. "Are you sure that's all?"

Tyson nodded, his lower lip trembling. "My head hurts," he moaned.

"Okay, bud. You go lie down on the couch." Paul ran cold water over a washcloth while his mind raced. He hurried back to the boy's side.

"Tyson, has anyone ever told you if you're allergic to anything?" Paul asked.

Tyson nodded, but looked even more fretful as he tried to recall details.

Paul took a deep breath. "Okay," he said. "You just stay here and try to relax. I'm—" what was he going to do? "—I'm going to go make a phone call."

It suddenly occurred to him that Charlotte must know if Tyson was allergic to anything.

As his teacher, it would be vital for her to have that information.

He rapidly punched in Charlotte's number and breathed a sigh of relief when she answered right away. He nervously told her about Tyson's symptoms.

"It's going to be okay, Paul," she said. Comfort washed over him at the sound of her voice. "Try to find some of his anti-allergy medicine if you can."

"I don't think I have any," Paul said, cringing as he omitted the fact that he wouldn't know whether he did or not.

"That's okay," Charlotte said. "I've got some. I keep it in case something happens in the classroom. I'll be right over."

Paul thanked her and disconnected, then went to check on Tyson.

His cheeks were still spotty and flushed, and he looked anxious, but he was breathing normally.

"Ms. Connelly is coming over with some medicine to make you feel better."

"My teacher?" But Tyson's interest was listless at best. It was plain he really wasn't feeling well.

A few minutes later, there was a knock at the door. When Paul opened it, there stood

Charlotte in the periwinkle sweater she wore that brought out her remarkable eyes.

"Where is he?" she asked. He led her to the couch.

Charlotte sat down on the edge of the couch beside him. "Hi, Tyson. So you're feeling kind of rotten?"

The little boy nodded. "I feel hot and itchy."

"We'll get you better, I promise." She took a small bottle out of her purse and coaxed Tyson to open his mouth and accept two droppers full of the liquid.

"Now you just lie back down and try to relax," Charlotte said. "The redness and itching will start to go away soon." She looked up at Paul. "What was the last thing Tyson ate?"

"Some pineapple."

"Tyson is allergic to pineapple." Her tone wasn't accusatory, but it was puzzled. "Didn't anyone tell you?"

Paul hesitated. "I might have heard, but…" He could hear the nervousness in his own voice.

Charlotte put her hand over his in a reassuring gesture. "You've had a lot to adjust to," she said. "Look, why don't I make you a list that you can put up on the fridge? Things like what to do if Tyson ever has another reaction, phone numbers you should have handy, that kind of thing."

"That's not necessary," Paul said, hating that he had to push her away when every part of him screamed that he needed her help. But what was the point of her making a list that he wouldn't be able to read?

"I was just caught off guard," he said. "I'll know what to do next time. I really do appreciate you coming over." He touched her arm and felt its warmth beneath the softness of the sweater.

She raised her eyes to his with a question that suddenly seemed to be about more than Tyson's allergies. But he couldn't let her get too close. He stepped back, and for a moment she looked as entirely abandoned as he often felt.

"Well... I'll leave this for you anyway," Charlotte held up the bottle. "I can pick up some extra for school on the way home." She handed the bottle to Paul. "The instructions are on the back."

He held it in his hand, not looking at it. "Thank you again for coming over."

"Paul...if there's anything else I can do? Anything at all..."

There was that feeling again, like she could see right through him. He shrugged it off.

"No, everything is fine now," he said. "I'll walk you to the door and then I'd better get Tyson to bed."

Charlotte hesitated at the door. "If you're sure…"

"I'm sure," he told her. "Thank you so much again. Have a good night."

Later, as he sat by Tyson's bedside, Paul thought about the near miss they'd just had, and he worried about a real emergency. Oh, he knew how to dial 911, but the thought of it coming to that terrified him.

For the first time since he had shared his secret with his sister, Erica, when they were teenagers, Paul gave serious consideration to telling someone else the truth about his illiteracy.

And the first person that came to mind was Charlotte Connelly.

Chapter Seven

At the end of September, on a Tuesday, Charlotte was leaving school with her head filled with more than what was going on in the classroom. She had finished up her lessons on pets by asking the students to draw pictures of pets they owned or wished they did. Choices ranged from kittens to dragons and, as she had predicted, Tyson drew a dog with floppy ears, grinning teeth and a lolling tongue.

She had not raised the subject of overseas missionary work with her parents since their phone call and, although she knew she would have to address it when she saw them again, for the time being her mind was focused on the matter of her and Paul meeting with the church council to present his idea of teaching basic car and home maintenance skills to the newcomers and whoever else was interested.

For a reason she couldn't pinpoint, or didn't want to admit to, it was important to her that the council agree to Paul's plan. She wanted him to feel welcome, like he had purpose, and she admitted to herself that she was looking forward to the additional contact she would have with him.

Feeling jittery, Charlotte hardly ate anything before heading over to the church. When she entered, she kept her eyes open for Paul—Tyson was staying at Mildred's for the duration of the meeting—and she spotted him almost immediately, pacing and looking as anxious as she felt.

She approached him and suppressed a sudden urge to offer a reassuring hug.

"Ready?" she asked.

"As I'll ever be."

"It's a good idea, Paul. It really is. I'm sure they'll see that."

They went to the meeting room and sat across the large table from one another. Soon the council members, consisting of Ralph Meyer, Joe Rockaberry, Olivia Meissner, Seth and Rena Acoose, and Dudley Bowen from the pharmacy filed in and took their seats.

After an opening prayer and some introductory remarks by Joe, who was the chairman for the year, Paul was invited to share his request with the council.

Charlotte offered up a quick, silent prayer that he would find the right words.

"As you know, there is a group of people who meet at the church on Wednesday nights to learn how to read and improve their English-speaking skills," Paul said. His unease was obvious at first, but as he warmed to his subject, Paul began to speak with more confidence. "You also know that I work at Harold's Garage and I'm pretty handy at repairs in general. So, as I told Charlotte, I got to thinking that there are other skills that I could teach—just basic things like checking the oil in a car or fixing a leaky faucet. It's amazing how much confidence it gives a person to feel independent in those ways. I believe it would make a real difference for them."

Charlotte saw Olivia Meissner raise her eyes from the notes she had been making and scrutinize Paul for a moment before glancing over at Charlotte. She tried to smile reassuringly at the older woman. Stone-faced, Mrs. Meissner turned her attention back to Paul.

"What about language barriers?" she asked.

"Well," Charlotte began to answer, "the literacy classes will continue, of course, and—"

"I believe I directed my question to Mr. Belvedere," Mrs. Meissner interjected.

Charlotte was anxious to see how Paul would handle the question. She watched him sit up straighter in his chair, and almost as if she was pulled by the same invisible magnet, Charlotte felt herself straightening her own shoulders.

"I teach by demonstration, Mrs. Meissner," Paul said. "It's all very visual and hands-on. I show people how to do things and then I supervise while they try it themselves."

"Paul has already helped me with some projects," Charlotte couldn't resist interrupting. "I can vouch that he's a good teacher." The look of appreciation he gave her across the table made her thankful that she had spoken up.

"Well, it sounds like that could work..." Mrs. Meissner said thoughtfully. "We'll be counting on your groups to work closely together, Charlotte, and possibly overlap."

"Of course." Charlotte nodded.

Finally a vote was taken, and it was agreed that they would give the fix-it classes a try, in conjunction with the literacy group. Paul and Charlotte thanked the council. Then he caught her eye and gave her a wide-open grin that made her feel like she had been given a gift.

She tried to remind herself why she couldn't let herself be too attracted to Paul. She feared she was losing the battle, and she would have to pray about it later.

"I think that went pretty well, don't you?" Paul said as he and Charlotte walked out together.

"It did," she agreed. "You did great. I was pr—" She stopped herself, wondering if it was going too far to tell him she was proud of him.

But his eyes lit up with a gentle light and he asked, almost shyly, "You were proud of me?"

Oh boy... Charlotte blushed profusely. Paul glanced at his watch. "We wrapped up earlier than I expected, so Tyson's okay at Mildred's for another half hour. Could I buy you a cup of coffee at Seth's? We could talk about the class."

Unable to resist, Charlotte said, "I'd like that."

As always, Seth's was buzzing with customers, some enjoying a late supper, some killing time before heading to the movie theater, and many, like the two of them, just in to enjoy some coffee and conversation.

Charlotte glanced around and spotted Bridget

sitting at a table with Stephanie. She waved at them and ignored Bridget's raised-eyebrow question. She wouldn't know what answer to give anyway.

Paul's eyes followed the direction of her wave and he nodded at Bridget and Stephanie.

"Do you want to ask your cousin and Stephanie to join us?" he suggested.

"Oh, no, that's fine," Charlotte said hurriedly. "I mean, I appreciate the thought, but I'm sure they're busy chatting."

"Okay, if you're sure." Paul said. "You and Bridget seem close."

"We are. She's more like a sister to me than a cousin."

Eugenie appeared at their table, and Charlotte, mindful of the time of night, ordered a cup of lemon-ginger tea, while Paul opted for a cup of decaf.

"Anything to eat?" Eugenie offered. "Seth made cinnamon buns today."

"Don't torture me," Charlotte groaned. "I really shouldn't."

"Why don't we share one?" Paul suggested.

They agreed it was a good compromise and Eugenie nodded with satisfaction and went off to fill their order.

They settled back to bask in the success

of the meeting and Charlotte felt an attachment to Paul that she hadn't felt with anyone in a long time.

Eugenie brought their order over, and after a couple of bites Paul said, "You said that Bridget is like a sister to you. Are you an only child?"

There was the barest hint of hesitation and a look of something so fleeting he couldn't quite grasp it before Charlotte answered his question. "Yes, it's just my parents and me. But we do spend a lot of time with Bridget and her family. Our dads are brothers."

Charlotte chatted about some of the funny adventures and family occasions she and Bridget shared growing up. Paul was happy to sit back and listen to Charlotte talk about her family. Maybe one day, he would talk to her about his parents and his sister.

"I remember one particular Easter," Charlotte said. "I think we must have been around seven, and we hid out in Aunt Brenda's walk-in closet and completely devoured the big chocolate rabbits we'd been given. I can tell you that it wasn't pretty. To this day, I'll choose almost any kind of treat before chocolate."

"You don't like chocolate?" Paul queried.

Charlotte shook her head. "Not in the slightest."

Then she told a funny story about the swimming lessons she and Bridget had taken. "It was hard for Bridge to learn how to swim when she was determined to never get her hair wet."

The words made Paul glance in the direction of Charlotte's cousin and note that her hair and makeup looked perfect as always.

"You're not like that," he found himself saying out loud, thinking of how Charlotte went back and forth from prim to casual and that he liked both sides of her. "You don't always have to be perfect."

"I'll choose to take that as a compliment," Charlotte said with a twinkle in her extraordinary eyes.

Paul excused himself to call Mildred to see how Tyson was faring. "No need to rush," Mildred assured him. "You and Charlotte visit as long as you like." Paul thought she sounded highly pleased about the whole matter.

"Does Tyson want to talk to me?" he asked.

Mildred told him that Tyson and Max were busy playing pirates and she was making him walk the plank. Paul shook his head and chuckled. "Why am I not surprised?"

When he returned, he saw that Bridget was standing at their table chatting with Charlotte. She said hello to him and then went back to sit with Stephanie.

Paul sat down again and resisted the urge to ask Charlotte what they'd talked about.

"Mildred says that Tyson is fine. Max is over there, too."

"That Mildred is a trouper," Charlotte declared.

"Is that any way to talk about one of your students?" Paul gently chided her. Then as she blushed, he grinned at her and told her about the plank walking.

"Apparently Tyson is a trouper, too," she said, and they laughed together.

After some silence, in which Paul asked himself if he was imagining something between them, he said in a deliberately light tone, "So, we said we were going to talk more about the fix-it program."

"I'm so glad it's a go. And I'm glad I'll be here to see it get underway and to help the other volunteers blending the classes in case I…well, in case I end up leaving."

Paul sipped his coffee silently, unsure of what to say.

Reading his silence as disapproval, Charlotte said, "I do plan to finish up the school year."

All at once, the previous ease of their time together vanished. Paul felt bad about that, but it reminded him what his priorities were.

"I really should go pick up Tyson," he said.

Charlotte nodded, her eyes cast downward. Silently she drank what was left of her tea. Then she spoke.

"Paul, I'm not gone yet. I'm committed to helping Tyson have the best year in my classroom that he can have. And now we have this new program at the church that we'll work on together. Can't we focus on those things and not worry about the future?"

"I just like to be prepared," Paul said. "I've found in my life that it's better that way. That way people can't disappoint you."

"And I've noticed," Charlotte answered softly, "that there's no way you can prepare for everything that happens in life."

There was a sadness in her that made him wonder what she was referring to.

"Time to go." She stood up, and he followed suit.

"Thank you for the tea," Charlotte said. "Please say hello to Tyson for me and I'll see him tomorrow." She didn't include the fact that she would see Paul, too.

They parted ways in front of Seth's Café.

Despite her reassurance that she would be in town until June, and her urging for him to take life as it came, Paul was more determined than ever to make sure that he kept some distance between them, at least as far as his emotions went.

"I guess I'll see you in class tomorrow night," he said without the enthusiasm he'd felt earlier.

Charlotte nodded, and he tried not to notice her troubled look.

"I can tell you then how Tyson's day went, if you like," she said.

"I'd appreciate that."

They sounded so formal, Paul thought. It was like a gauzy curtain had been hung between them. They could still see and hear each other, but the feeling of closeness and comfort that was starting to develop had retreated again.

He was glad that he hadn't told her his secret.

Chapter Eight

Charlotte stood by Paul's side at the front of the classroom and felt decidedly out of place. Not only because she had as least as much to learn as anyone when it came to being handy, but also because of how she and Paul had parted ways the night before.

It had been easy to pinpoint the change in mood to when she mentioned going away to do missionary work. It was frustrating that he doubted her good intentions, but she didn't know what she could do about that.

She could see that Paul was in his element, smiling and gesturing and somehow managing to make "righty-tighty and lefty-loosey" sound like the most fun anyone could possibly want to have. He had a way of making the participants comfortable and encouraging them until they performed the task with ease, and he encouraged the others to applaud everyone's efforts.

Paul stepped closer to her. It both intrigued and troubled her that she was already familiar with his scent that mingled fresh laundry with the light sweat of good, honest work.

"Your turn," he said.

The expression in his eyes was complicated; it wasn't unfriendly, but it wasn't at ease, either. It gave her the sensation that he had as many questions as she did…and was just as afraid to ask them.

"You can't be the only one who doesn't try," he urged.

Charlotte shook away the thought that those words had more import than he meant them to have.

Eugenie caught her eye when Paul wasn't looking and waggled her eyebrows. Charlotte smiled a noncommittal smile. Honestly, people in this town were just too much sometimes. But she was glad she could hide her confused, flustered feeling behind her lack of coordination and blame the friendly ribbing of the group for the warmth in her cheeks.

When Charlotte finally succeeded in removing a bolt and then screwing it back in again, Paul led the group in applause, and she was both relieved that it was over and regretful that his praise felt so impersonal.

Please, Lord, she prayed silently, *help me to keep my focus.* She needed to think about helping the group and learning new skill sets, not what the particularly handsome instructor was doing.

When the class was over, she murmured that she was going to see if Stephanie needed any help cleaning up and hurried out of the room.

Stephanie and a couple of others were busy stacking chairs and wiping down tables. Charlotte grabbed a stack of books and carried them to the appropriate shelf.

"How was the fix-it class?" Stephanie asked.

"Good," Charlotte said. "Paul is a great teacher."

"And?" Stephanie prodded.

"And I hope we all learn some things that can help us out, including me."

"I hear Paul makes house calls, too," Stephanie said.

Charlotte knew she was teasing her, but she wasn't in the mood for it. She had enough distraction with her own conflicted thoughts. Nevertheless, she forced a smile.

"I'm pretty sure he would help out anyone who asked him," she said.

When they went out into the main area, she could see Paul squatted down beside Tyson, and ruffled his hair, making it stand up while Ty squirmed and alternated between protests and giggles.

"You look kinda funny," teased the ever-helpful Max.

"Yeah, you look really stupid," said Michael, with a biting edge that lacked a teasing tone.

Charlotte watched Paul stand up quickly, looking somehow larger than he already was. For a split second she could see the flash of true fight in his eye. But surely he would keep in mind that Michael was just a little boy—a troubled, unpleasant one, to be sure, but a little boy nonetheless.

Then she saw Paul almost visibly maintain his self-control.

"Come on, Ty," he said. "It's time to go."

As they walked toward the door, Charlotte could hear him gently coaching his nephew on the importance of ignoring the mean things that people said. It was the Paul she knew, the caring and encouraging uncle, and it was almost as if she had imagined what she had seen in his eyes a few minutes ago.

Except she knew she hadn't, and it made her even more curious about him.

His eyes briefly locked with hers as he and Tyson walked by, and he gave her a small wave. "Good job tonight, Charlotte," he said. She wondered why those simple words meant so much to her.

Michael's mother came from the direction of the library. She looked bleary-eyed and slightly rumpled, as she often did. Charlotte hesitated to approach the woman who gave off the vibe of not liking her, even though she didn't really know her. Then again, she didn't know the woman, either. But they were called by the Lord to be a welcoming community, and if the woman couldn't find acceptance at a church, where could she?

Charlotte took a deep breath and made herself walk over. "Hi there!" she said with a confidence that she didn't feel. "My name's Charlotte Connelly, and I think I heard you're Mavis Cannon? And I know Michael because I have friends who help with the children here."

She held out her hand. Mavis studied it with an expression like Charlotte was about to release a toxic substance, then she briefly shook the extended hand, dropping it quickly. Her hand felt cold.

"Don't just stand there, Mikey. Say hello," Mavis ordered her son, who suddenly looked small and not like a bully. He mumbled something that could have been a hello.

"I've noticed you both here before," Charlotte forged ahead, "and I want you to know that you're welcome to join in any of the groups, or if you need help with—"

"What I need is peace and quiet," Mavis cut her off. "Which is exactly why I don't join any of the groups."

"Oh…well…" Charlotte floundered.

"Look," Mavis said, "I'm sure you mean well, everyone does. But none of you get it."

Briefly Charlotte thought about asking if the other woman wanted to explain, but Mavis had already made it clear that she didn't want questions.

"Say, you're the schoolteacher, right?" Mavis asked suddenly, tilting her head in a speculative way. "What grade do you teach?"

"I teach grade one."

"Well, maybe you and Mikey here will have the chance to get to know each other better. If things work out with the rental place I'm after, I think we might be moving here."

Her teaching experience helped Charlotte keep her expression neutral, although her thoughts immediately flew to Tyson and what Paul would think if Michael ended up in the same classroom.

"I'll look forward to that." She smiled at the boy, who scowled.

On her way home, Charlotte wondered if she should say anything to Paul about the possibility of Tyson and Michael being class-mates. But she realized that professionally, it wasn't her place to reveal what the plans of another family might be.

If only that fact would appease her con-science.

On Thursday morning Paul took advantage of the pre-lunchtime lull at the garage to clean up his work area. He hoped the routine mo-notony of the work would be enough to chase away the troublesome thoughts that coursed through him. He was worried about the way Michael treated Tyson and was thankful that his nephew didn't have to see the other boy on a daily basis. He wondered if they should stop attending the Wednesday night gather-ings, but quickly dismissed that idea. Tyson enjoyed it there for the most part, and he had made a commitment to the fix-it class partic-ipants, which he intended to follow through on. He was also starting to enjoy the cama-raderie at church.

He thought of Charlotte and how funny and shy she'd been when it was her turn. He enjoyed seeing her on Wednesday nights, too. There was nothing wrong with admitting that to himself. She was a good person, and she was Tyson's teacher.

And the way she fumbled with the screwdriver made him want to place his hand over hers and help her.

Don't go there, he warned himself.

The chime of the door snapped him out of the direction that his thoughts were headed in, which was probably a good thing. Except when he saw that the customer who'd come in was Charlotte.

"Back again?" he quipped.

"Well, I'm assisting with a simple home- and car-repair class," she said, bantering back. "And the instructor seems like a bit of a stickler, so I figured I'd better make sure I have everything I need."

"A stickler, you say? I can't possibly imagine." They both grinned at each other.

Then they chitchatted about what Charlotte's class was busy with that morning as Paul helped her find the items she was looking for. He rang them up quickly on the cash register.

"Good memory," she commented.

"Pardon?"

"The prices. You rang everything up without looking. Harold's cash register is old-school and doesn't have a scanner."

"Oh, right. Well… I just find it's easier to remember them. Makes things go faster in the long run."

He couldn't tell her what a painstaking process it was, constantly committing prices to memory, and the casual way he had to ask things like, "What are boxes of these nails going for again?" There were always tricks when a person couldn't read. It was utterly exhausting.

But the most exhausting thing of all was keeping the secret.

Just as Paul was placing Charlotte's purchases in a bag, Harold came into the shop, bringing in a rush of fresh autumn air with him.

"Hi, Harold," Charlotte greeted him.

"Hey there, Charlotte," he said, his words sounding a bit peculiar.

"Ah, I'm guessing you've been at the dentist."

The older man nodded with pained resignation.

"Get going for your lunch," he slurred at Paul. "You covered for me while I was out. You can walk this pretty lady back to school."

Paul glanced at Charlotte, and something in her eyes unsettled him.

"You don't have to," she said. "I mean, if you're busy."

"No, it's all good. Harold's right, I could use a break."

"Take your time," Harold urged with his lopsided grin.

"I get spoiled always knowing when my lunch break is going to be," Charlotte remarked as they headed toward the school. "I guess for you it depends on how busy you are."

"It usually works out," Paul said. "Harold's fair that way, like just now."

"Harold's a good guy."

Paul noticed that they had both chosen to ignore the "pretty lady" comment.

"Do you have any special plans for Thanksgiving?" Charlotte asked. "I'm already planning art projects for the kids. It will be here sooner than we think." Then, as if realizing that the question might remind him of the loss of Tyson's parents, before he could reply, she spoke of her own plans with family.

"Of course," she said, with a nervous little laugh, "we have so many family meals together, it's hard to know sometimes what makes Thanksgiving different than any other get-together."

"The turkey?" Paul suggested.

"Maybe."

"It'll just be Ty and me," he said, returning to her original question. "But we always manage to enjoy ourselves."

"You know, Paul, you and Tyson are more than welcome to join us…"

"I appreciate that," he said. "But, you know, I think it's better if we are on our own this year. Tyson has done remarkably well adjusting, but it's still pretty hard on both of us, and special occasions can be especially tough. Besides, it's still a few weeks away, and I wouldn't want you to feel tied down to the invitation."

"Of course," Charlotte said. "I'm sorry."

"Don't be. I know you meant well."

For a moment they were silent, then Charlotte changed the subject. "I talked to Mavis a bit after you left last week."

"Michael's mom?"

"Yes."

He had the feeling that she wanted to tell him something.

"How did it go?" he prompted.

"Good… I mean, okay. She's not very friendly, but I don't think she's a bad person.

I think she's been through a lot and could use some support."

"Do you think you're the person to offer that?"

They had stopped at the gate of the fence that surrounded the school grounds. She tilted her head and fixed him with slightly challenging look.

"I think any of us can be the person to offer that to someone, don't you?"

"I suppose." He wasn't about to tell her that he rarely believed in the inherent goodness of people or in their ability to help others.

"Have you ever read *To Kill a Mockingbird*?" Charlotte asked. "It's one of my all-time favorite books. I just love what it says about decency and the human spirit, and the ways that people can be more than what we expect them to be."

"And less," Paul couldn't help adding, thankful that he had seen the movie, which was said to be a fine representation of the book. "I mean, there's no denying that Atticus Finch is a noble guy, but the prejudices in that town were appalling. I'm not sure what's so uplifting about that."

"Well, I guess we'll have to debate that another time," Charlotte said. "Thanks for walking with me."

As she turned to go, the heel of her shoe caught on some gravel and she lost her balance.

Paul caught her by the elbow as her knees buckled and she started going down. He steadied her, and she was fine. He could let go.

Except he didn't want to…

Her cheeks were flushed such an appealing shade of pink that reminded him of the way the apple blossoms used to look on the tree in his parents' backyard before the apples came. She smelled so good—not the overpowering scent of perfume, but the smell of soap and crisp autumn air.

Before he knew what he was doing, he bent his head and placed a soft kiss on Charlotte's mouth.

Chapter Nine

Charlotte spent the afternoon with her thoughts in a haze, grateful that her students were engaged in silent reading time. She was glad she didn't have to say much, because she kept having the most inappropriate urge to blurt out, "Paul Belvedere kissed me!"

She didn't know how she felt about it—it had happened so quickly and so unexpectedly. But, by the look on his face afterward, she could tell that Paul was as puzzled by what had happened as she was. He had mumbled something about getting back to the shop before hurrying away, which caused her to feel even more confused. She had been completely caught off guard, but he didn't need to act like he could hardly wait to get away from her.

After school, she met up with Bridget at

Seth's Café. She hadn't been in the mood to go home. And Bridget usually had good insights, although she might make too much out of it. Still, Charlotte decided she was willing to risk it if only to find a way to deal with the unsettled feelings that were coming over her.

"He *what*?" Bridget shrieked, causing Charlotte to immediately regret seeing her cousin.

"Bridge," Charlotte warned, glancing around to see what kind of attention her cousin's outburst had brought. "Please don't make me sorry that I told you."

"Sorry." Bridget lowered her own voice. "But, really, Char, this is kind of a big deal. How do *you* feel about it?"

Charlotte didn't respond to that. There wasn't any point, because it would only lead to talk about obligations and family, and would lead her thoughts to Anna, the one person she wanted most to talk about, the one person no one ever wanted her to mention.

"I don't know how I feel," she admitted, suddenly afraid that telling Bridget had stirred up more questions than it was going to answer.

"You like him, though, right?" Bridget prodded. "I mean, I can think of a lot worse things in the world than being kissed by Paul Belvedere."

"He's a nice enough guy," Charlotte said. She wasn't going to try to explain the jolt she had experienced when their lips had touched.

"I guess I'm making the choice not to over-analyze it," she finally said, knowing it was a cop-out. "I have other things on my mind. I have to complete the application for that missionary work position, for one thing."

"You haven't filled that out yet?" Bridget said, surprised. "You're usually so on top of things. Char, are you sure your heart is really in it?"

"It is. It's such a good cause. Maybe I just want to make sure I do everything right. I do know I want to do more with my life."

"But not romance?" For all her breezy exterior, Bridget did have a way of getting to the point.

Charlotte was spared having to answer by the appearance of Seth at their table with a pot of coffee.

"How's your evening, ladies?" he asked. "Some more decaf for you?"

After they had exchanged a few pleasantries and turned down the tempting offer of apple pie, Seth continued on to the next table and Charlotte took the opportunity to steer the conversation in another direction.

"Have you heard that Mavis is looking to rent an apartment here in town?"

"No, I hadn't heard that. I still wonder what the deal with them is."

"I don't really know. I have the feeling they're coming out of a bad situation. Anyway, I hope they find whatever it is they're looking for." Charlotte couldn't put it into words exactly, but she meant more than just a place to live.

"I hope so, too," Bridget said. "Listen, Char, I've been meaning to tell you, Mom says that she's worried your mom's health is getting worse."

"I know," Charlotte said. "Dad has been worried, too. I've been trying to check in with her more often. Thanks for letting me know."

Charlotte felt slightly ashamed of herself. Sometimes she forgot that, for all of her interest in fashion and dating, there was a sensitive and observant side to Bridget, too.

She took a sip of her coffee and felt a sudden pulse of awareness, then she realized that Paul was standing beside their table. It was only natural that others in the café would be aware of it, too, but he didn't seem to care and didn't even greet Bridget before saying, "I need to talk to you. Can you come outside with me, please?"

Paul saw Charlotte dart a quick glance at Bridget, who gave a little shrug. At first she didn't move, but just as he was wondering if he would have to ask her again, Charlotte followed him outside.

They took a few steps away from the café entrance so that they weren't blocking it and they were also away from the gazes of the café customers.

"I just…wanted to apologize for what happened earlier," Paul said. "I truly don't know what got into me."

Charlotte wasn't quite able to look at him, and her appealing bashfulness caused an inner struggle not to take her in his arms and kiss her again.

"I wasn't upset," she said, "just caught off guard. I wasn't exactly sure what to think, but…" Her violet eyes swept up to his and nearly undid him. "I thought about it most of the afternoon."

"You did?" The idea of that shouldn't please him, not when he'd come to make amends. But it did.

"Don't worry," Charlotte said, "I didn't neglect the students."

"I'm not worried." Strangely, he realized that he hadn't been worried about Tyson's day. His thoughts had been preoccupied with other things.

"Where is Tyson?" Charlotte asked.

"He's at a playdate at Max's. I'm on my way to get him."

"I'd better get back inside," Charlotte said. "You know the rumor mill will really be churning now."

They exchanged smiles of acknowledgment.

But instead of going back inside the café, she lingered, and he had the impression that she was in no rush to end their time together. He didn't want it to end, either. He checked the time.

"Could I... I mean, would you mind if I joined you? I have time before I have to pick up Ty."

"Are you willing to risk the gossip?" It was a joke, but there was a real question behind it, too.

"I'll risk it," he said.

It felt easy and natural to sit with Charlotte and Bridget as they chatted. They didn't put pressure on him to say much, which he appreciated, and he was glad of the opportunity to get to know more about Charlotte.

Some of their conversation focused on church, but only in the way that it was a natural part of their lives, so for the first time in forever, he wasn't uneasy with a faith-based conversation.

There had been a time in his life when he had enjoyed church and believed that he could find hope there. To live life without faith in anything was feeling less and less like a good option. Maybe it was time that he considered inviting God back in.

Chapter Ten

Charlotte faced the rest of the week feeling more settled. It had been a pleasant surprise when Paul had asked to join her and Bridget for coffee at Seth's. She hoped that he was starting to feel like a part of the community. But still, the memory of their kiss lingered, and she questioned exactly why it was so important to her that he feel at home in Green Valley.

Bridget, to her credit, hadn't bombarded her with questions when Paul had finally left the café to pick up Tyson. She'd just noted that she thought he was a nice guy.

For Charlotte, it didn't matter one way or the other, because she wasn't looking for anything right now.

Though it was becoming more difficult to convince herself that was true.

The next day on her lunch break, Charlotte found a quiet place and phoned her mother.

"Hi, Mom, how are you doing today? I just wanted to say hi."

"How nice of you to make time to check in, Charlotte," her mom said. "I heard you had coffee with your cousin last night. It's good when you girls can get together."

Though there was nothing amiss in the words, Charlotte felt a slight twinge of the perpetual guilt that hounded her.

"Have you had any updates from the doctors?" she asked.

Her mother sighed wearily. "No, but I'm becoming increasingly convinced that these doctors aren't worth much. I've even had your father take me to a specialist in Regina, and they can't pinpoint a cause. But there has to be some reason why I feel so unwell most of the time."

"Have you considered that it could be stress?" Charlotte asked cautiously. "Both Dad and I want you to slow down and stop thinking you have to serve on every committee that comes along."

"Now you sound just like those ridiculous doctors," her mother huffed. "I'm not just some silly woman who doesn't know anything about my own health."

Charlotte took a deep breath, closed her eyes briefly and opened them again.

"I know, Mom. Listen, I have some things to do, but I can pop by later and we can talk more about it."

"I don't want to put you out of your way."

"You're not. I'll talk to you later." Charlotte snapped off her phone.

She decided to use what remained of her lunch break to walk to Dudley's and buy an envelope and a stamp. It was time to mail out her application before she allowed doubts and demands to overcome her.

But she didn't have the feeling of satisfaction she'd been hoping for when the envelope slipped from her fingers into the post office box. She hoped that she was headed to a place where she could make a difference and not simply running away from her responsibilities here.

During afternoon recess, Rena popped her head into her classroom and said, "Hi. I just saw Mr. Millis, and he asked if you can see him after school."

Charlotte looked up from the spelling tests she was marking and nodded briefly. She was distracted by a troubling number of mistakes on Tyson's test. She'd thought he was making progress, but now she wasn't so sure. She would have to keep an eye on things and see if additional tutoring was needed. She would mention it to Paul, too, as soon as she could.

Then, like a delayed reaction, she wondered why the principal wanted to see her.

"Did he say what it was about?"

"Nothing too pressing," Rena said. "I think you're getting a new student in your classroom next week."

"Okay," she said. "Thanks, Rena."

It had to be Michael. She was sure of it, and she worried about the potential impact. Not just in her classroom but in her relationship with Paul.

It took Paul time to realize that the unfamiliar feeling he was experiencing was happiness. He could not remember the last time he had even considered letting his guard down and becoming part of a community. But now he knew it was because of Charlotte and the kind of comfort and trust he felt when he was around her.

Since he had managed to squeak through high school and graduate, he had wanted nothing more than to be invisible. So he had chosen to live in larger cities where he could avoid getting close to anyone and could leave at a moment's notice when others got too close and asked too many questions.

All that had changed with the tragic deaths of Erica and Ross, and being suddenly thrust into the role of Tyson's guardian. For Tyson's sake he was willing to make changes to his life, but he had never considered before that such changes could be good for him, too. He loved teaching the classes at the church's community center; it gave him a feeling of purpose and accomplishment. As far as he knew, Tyson had no complaints at school, but he trusted that Charlotte would let him know if he did.

At night, after he had tucked his nephew in and gotten ready for bed himself, he felt something rising up within him: not a prayer, exactly, but the slightest inclination to start talking to God again.

He enjoyed the way Charlotte had taken up the habit of popping into the garage on her lunch hour to show him new items she had bought for her house and he liked to banter with her over her purchases.

Sometimes she popped in simply to chat. Those were his favorite times of all.

The days passed in this pleasant way and September came to an end. On a Tuesday early in October, the lunch hour came and went and there was no sign of Charlotte. Paul told himself not to overreact. Her visits were something that he looked forward to, but that didn't mean he had the right to expect them.

Still, he had to focus on the other customers and not let his eyes keeping straying to the door or experience a jolt of anticipation each time the bell signaled that someone else had come into the garage.

He particularly had to stifle disappointment when the bell ushered in Olivia Meissner. He'd managed to steer clear of her as much as possible in a town the size of Green Valley. She made him feel like she could see all of his secrets.

"How was your weekend?" he asked her, mindful of customer service, while at the same time fervently hoping that she didn't have a complicated request of some kind.

"It was fine," she replied tersely. "My daughter-in-law cooked Sunday dinner, which was nice for a change."

Mrs. Meissner had just come in to pick up a couple of car air fresheners, which to his relief, Paul was readily able to assist her with. She took them and was quickly on her way.

Although brief and not exactly unpleasant, the encounter had nonetheless left Paul feeling exhausted. He realized that he was starting to count on Charlotte to add some light to his day, and when she didn't show up, it was a good reminder to him not to depend on anyone.

Besides, the months before she left for her mission work would speed by and then she'd be gone. It was best to face facts and start getting used to her being gone.

"Are you okay?" Harold asked him as he was preparing to leave to pick Tyson up from school. "You seem a bit off today. Don't get me wrong," he hurried to reassure Paul. "No complaints about your work. It just looks like something's bothering you."

"I think I'm just a little tired," Paul said. "And run-down. I might be catching one of those colds going around."

"Or maybe you're wondering where that pretty schoolteacher is today?"

Paul looked at Harold, but there was nothing in the older man's face but kindness and encouragement.

Still, he wasn't sure how he felt about his own expectations, let alone the opinions of others, no matter how well intentioned they might be. So, he simply said, "No, I'm just tired. If you need me back for anything, I can drop Ty off at Mildred's and come back."

"Nope, I'm good. Go home, rest up."

Paul had developed the habit of waiting for Tyson right outside the classroom door. At first it was because he felt protective and never wanted his nephew to worry that he wouldn't show up. He still felt that way, but now there was the added incentive of being able to chat with Charlotte. He loved hearing the way she spoke to the children that let them know she expected the best from them and was going to be patient until they reached that point.

Today, however, still feeling as if things weren't quite right, he lingered a bit farther down the hallway, making sure to keep an eye out in case Tyson didn't spot him right away.

The bell rang, and soon children started to stream out into the hallways, laughing and jostling one another despite the warnings from the teachers to be orderly. He spotted Rena and resisted the urge to ask her if she knew what Charlotte had done on her lunch break.

Then he saw Tyson and waved so that he would see him. The little boy headed toward him without the usual spring in his steps. Apparently, it was an off day for everyone. Then, Paul was unpleasantly surprised to see a sullen-looking boy following a few steps behind Tyson.

Michael.

Well, that explains it, he thought grimly. Charlotte was avoiding him because she knew he would be upset that Michael was now in Tyson's class and she hadn't said a word to him about it.

The logical part of him knew that Charlotte had no obligation to discuss her students with him, but he couldn't help wishing that she felt their friendship had warranted her mentioning it.

Chapter Eleven

As they walked home together, Paul asked Tyson, "How was school?" He didn't want to say anything about Michael, but he hoped Ty would raise the topic on his own.

"Okay, I guess."

"Anything new?" he prompted cautiously.

Tyson shrugged. "What's for supper?" he asked.

"Burgers and a salad. You can toss the salad."

Paul waited but Tyson just said, "Okay," and when their house was in sight, he ran ahead, causing his backpack to bounce up and down in time with his steps.

He jumped and squirmed on the doorstep while Paul unlocked the house.

"I haveta go to the bathroom," he said and made a mad dash as soon as the door was open.

"Really?" Paul said dryly. "I couldn't tell."

Maybe he was reading too much into things, he mused while he got out ingredients for the salad and waited for Tyson to come into the kitchen. Maybe it was only the need for the bathroom that had caused his nephew to seem anxious.

"Did you wash your hands?" he asked automatically when Tyson came back into the kitchen.

"You always ask me that!" Tyson protested, but he held his hands up for inspection.

"Good job, bud." Paul pulled a stool over to the counter and lifted Tyson up, then ran a bit of water into the sink and got him busy rinsing off the lettuce. Then he opened the fridge and took out the plastic wrap–covered tray that held the hamburger patties he had made earlier. He put a pan on the stove on medium heat and placed the patties into the pan. As they began to sizzle, he tried one more time to see if Tyson would say anything about his new classmate.

"So, how are the other kids at school? Lots of fun at recess?"

"Me and Max can't wait until it snows," Tyson said. "We're gonna see who can build the biggest snowman."

If Tyson was able to focus on his friends

and not on one boy that he didn't get along with, he could do the same.

"Maybe Max could come over after supper," he suggested. "If it's okay with her parents. Then you could help me rake up some leaves and jump in the piles. What do you say?"

"I say yes!" Tyson shouted enthusiastically. He resumed washing lettuce with added vigor, and Paul stopped him just in time from adding dish soap.

Paul breathed a sigh of relief. The idea actually took care of two things: although the more pressing one was ensuring that Tyson stayed happy, the Hansens had been good enough to invite Tyson over to play with Max a number of times, sometimes when Paul had other things to do, and he wanted to make sure that he extended the hospitality in return.

Shortly after they'd finished their supper, the doorbell rang and Tyson ran to the door.

"I'll be back to pick Max up in a couple of hours, if that's okay," the little girl's mother said.

"That's just fine," Paul agreed. He was happy to provide some diversion for Tyson and to try to get himself out of his own head.

Besides, he enjoyed Max, with her little-girl face and her funny, low voice. He suspected she kept Tyson on his toes…just like Charlotte did for him.

His fast-growing fondness for her was at war with his irritation and disappointment.

"Let's go." He ushered both kids outside.

Autumn had been Erica's favorite season, and the display of golden, brown and red leaves, as well as the distinctly crisp scent of another summer gone and the pending winter, reminded Paul of his sister. A wave of grief edged to the shore but was held back by Max's sudden burst of laughter and Tyson's higher-pitched giggle. He smiled and handed Max a rake.

"One for you."

"And here's one for you, bud." He handed another one to Tyson.

He wondered what Charlotte's favorite season was.

"Let's trade," Max said immediately, with the assurance of one who expected no arguments.

"Why?" Tyson asked.

"Because I like yours better," she said, as if stating the obvious.

Tyson threw a look in his uncle's direction. Paul laughed and put his palms up as if to say *don't look at me.*

Seconds later, they began raking leaves

into big piles with Max offering plenty of instruction along the way. As they raked and chatted, Paul kept his ears open in case either of them said anything about Michael… or their teacher. But all they talked about was their plans to build snowmen and go ice-skating in the winter.

"I'll teach ya how to do spins," Max promised.

Finally, when the piles of leaves were big enough, they took turns jumping into them. Paul knew he'd have to rake all the leaves up all over again, but it was worth it to see Tyson and Max having fun.

He was also glad that the stress of Thanksgiving had been taken care of with an invitation to join Harold and his brood, along with Mildred. They were relaxing people to be with, and he was happy that he and Tyson wouldn't be alone for Thanksgiving after all. He'd decided it was better than being alone and dwelling on who was no longer there.

He knew that Charlotte was preoccupied with her own family's expectations, but he recalled that she had extended an invitation and he wondered what Thanksgiving with her family would be like. It just felt easier, though, to be with Harold's family.

"If you come inside now," he said, "there's

just enough time for some hot cocoa and cookies before Max's mom picks her up."

While Tyson and Max competed to see who could get the best chocolate mustache, Paul felt his concerns creeping in again. He told himself that he shouldn't borrow trouble if there was no sign of any, but he kept returning to the thought that Charlotte should have said something to him about Michael.

"Look, I'm a chipmunk!" Max had stuffed her cheeks with mini marshmallows, which caused Tyson to hold his stomach as gales of laughter overtook him.

See, he's fine, everything's good, Paul told himself. But still, he couldn't get to sleep that night without promising himself that he'd talk to Charlotte about his concerns at the earliest possible opportunity.

Charlotte woke up on Wednesday morning still feeling like she was keeping important information a secret from Paul. *Please, God, help me deal with whatever this day is going to bring and help me not to expect the worst. Give me peace of heart and mind.*

But the prayer didn't get rid of the feeling of foreboding the way she'd hoped it would.

It had felt so odd not to visit with Paul on her lunch hour. And even worse because she knew why she was avoiding him, which was silly, because she was bound to run into him that night at the church if not before.

Despite her experience teaching and her determination to find the best in each student, she'd experienced a stab of apprehension when Michael was brought into her classroom.

The uneasiness continued so she wasn't all that surprised when Paul was waiting to talk to her after class. "I've made arrangements for Tyson to go home with Max and her parents for a little while," he said. "You and I need to talk."

She didn't bother to ask about what, just nodded and said, "You can come in and have a seat when the students have gone." She wished that he didn't look quite so large and male and intense. She was beginning to enjoy the smells of garage oil and gasoline…

Once they were settled in the classroom, Paul didn't waste any time getting to the point.

"You should have told me that Michael was going to be in your classroom."

His reprimanding tone reminded Charlotte that she wasn't a young woman with a developing crush; she was an education professional with her own set of ethics to protect.

She dismissed thoughts of how attractive Paul was to her now and answered in the crisp, no-nonsense voice she reserved for particularly challenging parents.

"It's not my business to discuss the plans of another student and their family with anyone else. I'm sure you wouldn't appreciate it if I discussed Tyson with another parent."

Paul shifted and frowned as if he was pondering her words.

"I suppose you're right," he said grudgingly. "I mean, in general terms, I can see what you mean. But you know that Michael has picked on Tyson in other situations. And besides… I thought we were friends."

The declaration of friendship under these circumstances irritated Charlotte. Perhaps it was the burden of her parents' expectations that weighed on her, but she felt especially weary of the tangled knots that seemed destined to go along with all of her relationships.

"I think," she said tightly, "that a friend wouldn't pressure another friend to do anything that put her in conflict with her professional ethics."

"I don't mean to," Paul said, looking disconcerted. "It's just…there's a lot about me that you don't know."

The shadowing in his dark eyes made Charlotte soften somewhat.

"Do you want to tell me about it?" she asked.

Briefly, he looked like he was considering it, but then he shook his head. "No, it doesn't matter. I'm really only concerned with Tyson." He continued, "I get why you couldn't say anything, and I'm sorry for pushing you on it. But can you at least promise me that you'll keep an eye on things and tell me if there's anything to worry about?"

"I keep an eye on my classroom at all times," Charlotte said. "And I can promise you that appropriate measures will be taken if they are necessary."

Her thoughts went to the poor grade that Tyson had gotten on the last spelling test, but she reminded herself that she was going to wait to see if it was just a onetime thing before raising the alarm with Paul.

A storm brewed over his face, which told her that he wasn't entirely satisfied with her answer. She didn't like having to remain so detached—she was very fond of both Paul and Tyson—but it was the fair thing to do.

"Can I walk you out?" she asked, because there wasn't much else she could say.

"Trying to get rid of me?"

She was disconcerted at first but then saw the twinkle in his eye. It appeared that Paul was ready to be done with their teacher-parent roles, too, but she had to say one more thing.

"I hope I've made it clear, Paul, I won't tolerate being pressured about this. But, at the same time, I want you to trust me. Can you do that? I care about Tyson, just as I care about all of my students."

"I trust you," Paul said, but she couldn't escape a peculiar sensation that those words were unfamiliar in his mouth. "I, uh, missed you at lunch yesterday," he added, his tone gruff with confession.

I missed you, too...

She couldn't bring herself to say the words or to admit that she had stayed away to avoid the very confrontation they'd just had.

"I had a couple of things I needed to take care of," she said. That was true on any given day in the life of a busy schoolteacher, but she didn't volunteer that she'd spent her lunch break searching missionary sites and commanding herself not to have second thoughts... Just as she had willed herself not to give in and walk over to Harold's so that she could see Paul's face light up when she came in the door.

"Well…you were missed." Paul said it in a shy way that warmed her heart.

It was clear that he didn't want there to be tension between them any more than she did.

She suddenly wondered how it would go over if she was to start dating the guardian of one of her students.

Whoa, now where did that thought come from?

Despite the kiss they'd shared, Paul had never given her any indication that he had the time or inclination for a relationship. She still knew that his primary focus was Tyson and the role she played in the boy's life as his teacher. He had proven that again today, and she had been reminded of what her responsibilities were, not only to both of them, but also to her profession in general.

Besides, there was her mission-work application, making its way through the mail and waiting to bring back with it the answer to her future.

An answer that she was no longer sure she was ready for.

Chapter Twelve

The October air had a chill to it, but there was still no snow, much to Tyson's disappointment. Thankfully, that appeared to be the only thing in his life that was troubling him.

When Paul had approached Charlotte about the Michael situation, he hadn't been entirely satisfied with her response. But now he felt like the real question—the one he wasn't ready to confront—was what had bothered him the most about it: Did he really just want to protect Tyson, or did he want evidence that he meant more to Charlotte than just another parent or guardian? By necessity, he never let himself get too close to people, so why did it matter to him?

These days, even more than when Erica first died, he longed to be able to sit down

to have a conversation with her. There were
so many things he wanted to ask her about
Tyson, to make sure that he was doing things
right. He had always been the fun uncle, but
his visits had been brief on his way from one
place to another. Now he found himself wishing daily that he had paid more attention to
how his sister and brother-in-law had raised
Tyson.

That was only one of many reasons that
he had been astonished to find out that Erica
had chosen him to be Tyson's guardian. Even
worse, she had expressed that, although they
had drifted apart over the years, she trusted
that they had their foundation of faith in common and that Paul would do his utmost to
make sure that Tyson had a loving home.

Well, he was doing the latter, but his foundation of faith had been eroded bit by bit
by the cruelty of classmates and had been
destroyed completely when his sister and
brother-in-law were killed.

Except now Charlotte had him thinking
again about his faith. It wasn't that they had
even talked about it or come anywhere close
to having a faith-based conversation, other
than the natural flow of it in her conversation
with Bridget when he'd stayed at Seth's and
had coffee with them. But when he saw her

around the church and how she treated people and interacted with others, he could almost believe that it was possible for God to have a positive impact on a person's life…almost.

Meanwhile, the days took their regular rhythm. He took Tyson to school, then he went to work at the garage. Charlotte had resumed her lunchtime visits, which made him happy, thought he tried not to count on that happiness. If Ty wasn't playing with Max after school, he kept him busy with a few age-appropriate chores or let him help get supper ready by setting the table or by stirring something on the stove. He kept himself busy, too, as there was always some kind of an errand or repair that he could do, either for himself or someone else. It was important to him now that the community thought of him as someone they could count on, but he knew it wasn't only for the sake of his employment anymore. He liked seeing his efforts reflected in the shine of Charlotte Connelly's eyes.

Paul also anticipated the Wednesday night class. It was so much fun to witness the growing self-confidence of the students, and he loved seeing Charlotte learning alongside him, even as she did her part teaching, and growing in her own confidence.

One night when there was no doubt that

winter was hiding in the October air, getting ready to unleash itself, he asked the class, "Okay, who wants to tell me how often you should be changing your furnace filter and why it's important to make sure you get your furnace and ducts cleaned before winter really sets in?"

Several enthusiastic hands waved in the air. He caught Charlotte's eye, and they smiled at each other. The other people around them faded for a moment, until an excited voice snapped him back to the present.

"I know the answer, please, Mr. Paul."

"Kamar." He signaled to a young man with smiling dark eyes. "What do you think?"

Kamar answered, and Paul nodded and led the class in applause for the correct answer that was given. Their efforts to learn and their pride in doing so made him feel happy, and he was pleased that he could play a part in it.

And that he could share the experience with Charlotte.

It is more blessed to give than to receive. The familiar Scripture jumped into his head, surprising him. Perhaps he hadn't forgotten as much as he thought he had.

The feeling of camaraderie stayed with him after the class had ended and, unlike when he had first started coming to the community activities, he had no urge to rush away. Instead, he hoped that Tyson would want to stay longer, so that he could enjoy visiting with his students and with Charlotte.

As it happened, Tyson was in especially high spirits that night.

"Max and I tooked turns being David and Goliath," he said breathlessly. "I slingshotted a stone at her and she fell and then she did one at me and I fell."

"Sounds kind of violent," Paul observed.

"Uncle Paul, it was only pretend stones," Tyson explained with exasperated patience. "Besides, the story is in the Bible, everyone knows that."

"You're right. How silly of me."

He got Tyson settled in a group of children enjoying cookies and milk and couldn't help noting that Michael wasn't among the group.

He spotted Charlotte sipping water from a bottle and chatting with Stephanie and Bridget. He watched her toss back her head and laugh heartily at something Bridget said, and he found that he was oddly jealous for a moment, wanting to be the cause of the laughter that brought such light and joy to her face.

A face he couldn't believe he had ever thought plain.

It struck Paul again that Erica was part of

this community and had shared in its spirit. He had purposely avoided seeking out any memories of her from the people who had known her for fear of unleashing grief in him or Tyson. But now he considered that someday he might appreciate hearing what others remembered about her.

Charlotte turned her head and smiled at him, then turned back to say something to the other women and came over to him.

"It was a good class tonight, wasn't it?" she said.

He nodded. "Yes, I'm really happy with how things are going." He wondered if she would know that he was talking about more than the class. He found her so appealing when her hair looked soft and her smile was bright.

He scanned the room, suddenly anxious to change the subject. "I didn't see Michael or his mother here tonight, did you?"

"No," she said. Her puzzlement mirrored his, minus the relief. "But I was hoping they'd be here. I wanted to make sure that their move to town went okay and see if they needed anything."

Of course she would be concerned about them, because that was the kind of person she was. He felt guilty for not being as open-hearted, but the feeling played tug-of-war with a resentment he couldn't seem to help. Paul mentally shook his head. He had to stop getting in his own way.

"Don't look now," Charlotte said, "but I see Joe and Ralph headed in your direction. Do you want me to distract them while you make a run for it?"

He chuckled. "No, I appreciate the offer, but that's fine. I actually promised I'd catch up with them tonight."

It was the truth, although it had slipped his mind until now. He couldn't help it if it gave him an excuse to escape her and the inner struggle she'd unwittingly caused.

His emotions felt like a roller coaster when it came to Charlotte Connelly and he didn't know why he couldn't convince himself to stop wanting to get closer to her. What had started out as nothing more than ensuring that Tyson was safe and happy in class had developed into more, despite his best efforts to keep her at arm's length. He could only hope now that he would find a way to deal with her imminent departure for her mission work.

Paul could sure muddle her with his stop-and-go signals, Charlotte thought, exasperated. The previous evening at the church, one minute he had been obviously glad to be with her, chatting and joking around. The next minute, darkness had come into his eyes and he was all too happy to use Joe and Ralph as a reason to get away from her.

She knew he didn't care for Mavis and Michael, but he was the one who'd asked if she had seen them, and she had answered honestly. A hint of irritation poked at her. She didn't need his opinion or shows of dissatisfaction. She had enough to contend with as she dealt with her increasingly ambivalent feelings about going away on her mission work.

That decision absolutely had to be based on what her heart told her was best for her, and from any guidance she could gain through prayer. She couldn't let the questioning eyes of the strong but vulnerable bachelor cause her to stay.

Her phone rang suddenly, startling her because she didn't often get calls in the morning. She answered it somewhat warily, hoping that nothing was wrong.

"Char?"

It was Bridget, and she sounded chipper. Charlotte breathed a sigh of relief.

"Dr. Parson has to drive into Regina for an early appointment, so he asked if I could open the clinic this morning. Do you want company walking this morning?"

"I would love that," Charlotte said sincerely. They quickly made arrangements and met on the corner of Charlotte's street. Walking and listening to Bridge chat about whatever popped into her mind was exactly what she needed to get her mind off her troubles. And away from a certain car mechanic and handyman who occupied her thoughts far more than he should.

"Did you have fun at the church last night?" Charlotte asked. "It felt like an especially good night. The students love Paul."

"It was fun but exhausting," Bridget said. "Those kids are high energy, let me tell you."

"How was…" Charlotte stopped herself from asking directly about Tyson. "How were the kids?" she amended. "Other than energetic, I mean."

"Oh, you know, they're always lots of fun. They sure keep you on your toes."

"I'm sure they loved having you there."

"I saw you and Paul talking," Bridget said, touching on the very subject that Charlotte hoped to avoid.

"Yes…there were a lot of people there last night." She hoped that Bridget would take the hint and move on to another subject. But the next words out of her cousin's mouth reminded her that it wasn't exactly her style to let things go.

"It's pretty clear that he likes you," she said matter-of-factly. "Do you not see it?"

Not for the first time, Charlotte regretted having a face that gave so much away when color swept through it.

"Sometimes I think he does," she admitted, figuring there was no sense denying what Bridget was bound to pry out of her anyway. "But then I feel like something changes between us and he puts up his walls again."

"Do you want him to like you? Do you like him?"

Charlotte wanted to give her an honest answer, but her own feelings were in such a jumble that she didn't know what to say. Finally she just shrugged and said, "I don't think it really matters. I've sent away my application to go overseas, and I'm waiting to hear about that."

"Char, I don't think you should run away from something that might be what you've been looking for. I'm just saying…"

"I'm not running away."

She was relieved when they arrived at the vet clinic and had to part ways.

During the remaining walk to school, Charlotte tried praying to sort out her thoughts and figure out exactly what she did want, but the one persistent thought that kept returning was that she needed to discover herself and not live by the wishes and whims of others.

But the words that Bridget had said about Paul liking her also landed like a timid sparrow on a wintry branch and clung in her mind with the same unexpected tenacity.

When Charlotte stepped into the schoolyard, her teacher's radar immediately flared up when she saw a cluster of children all focused on something that was happening in the midst of them. She hurried over. "What's going on?"

"Tyson punched Michael," a little girl named Raquel announced with self-importance.

"In the mouth," added another student.

"Tyson…?" Charlotte's temples pulsed as she tried to sort out the statement.

Her presence caused the cluster of children to break up, and sure enough, although she could hardly believe the evidence of her own eyes, Tyson stood glaring at the bigger boy with his hands still in fists at his sides, while Michael, with a look of shock and anger, touched his fingers to his bloody lip.

Chapter Thirteen

"That can't be true" were the first words out of Paul's mouth when Charlotte phoned to tell him what had happened and explain that it was mandatory to meet with the children, along with their parents or guardians.

"I'm afraid it is."

He thought he could hear sadness behind Charlotte's professional tone. But he knew that whatever her personal feelings might be on the matter, she would follow the rules. He couldn't help admiring her for it, even though he knew it meant she couldn't choose sides.

He hoped that her calm professionalism would impact him. Despite his first, pained reaction, he hoped he would be able to listen to the facts rationally and sort out why it had happened and what he could do about it.

Dear God...

He could only get out the beginning of a prayer because he hadn't talked to God in so long. He could only hope that God understood that he needed Him now and wouldn't hold it against him.

He told Harold only that there had been an incident at the school and was grateful for his boss's discretion in not asking for details.

"Get going," Harold said. "Take all the time you need and let me know if I can help."

"I will, thanks." He doubted there was anything Harold could do, but it was kind of him to offer.

Paul couldn't decide if the distance to the school felt like the longest or the shortest journey of his life. He had always felt a keen desire to protect Tyson, not only because the little boy had lost his parents, but also because he knew from firsthand experience that children could be cruel and adults, despite their best intentions, could be oblivious. So, from the moment he had taken on Tyson's guardianship, he had made it his goal to ensure that his nephew was safe and happy. Always.

Not once had it ever entered his mind that Tyson could be the one to do the bullying. There had to be more to it, he thought.

When he arrived at the school, he headed

directly to the principal's office and saw that Mavis was already there. A single glance in her direction told him that she was prepared to do battle for her son.

He couldn't blame her for that.

Michael was sitting beside her but wouldn't look up from staring at his shoes. Tyson stood a little ways away from them, looking like he hardly knew what to do with his own body.

Paul went and leaned over to give him a quick hug.

When Tyson looked up at him, it was clear that he was miserable, and surprised at the show of support that his uncle had given him.

"We'll get to the bottom of this," he just had time to whisper before Charlotte arrived and ushered them in to take seats. Soon after, Mr. Millis arrived and said. "Ms. Connelly will handle this. I'm here to observe and to mediate only if necessary."

Mavis's eyes sent daggers in his direction. He couldn't pretend he didn't know how she felt. Since the day he took guardianship of Tyson, he had lived on constant alert for this scenario. He just hadn't expected the roles to be reversed.

"Would you like to start, Michael?" Charlotte said in a quiet but firm voice. "Tell us in your own words what happened." Then she glanced at his nephew. "You will get your turn to talk, Tyson, all right? We do ask that no one interrupts while the other person is talking. The no interrupting goes for the parents, too." Her eyes swept over Paul and Mavis. "When the boys have each had their say, we'll discuss how we feel this can be most effectively dealt with."

Mavis mumbled something under her breath, and it didn't take much imagination to guess what she thought the repercussion should be. Once again, Paul couldn't blame her. He would have given anything if his parents had been the type to rage like a mother bear on his behalf. But they had been tired from work, worried about bills, perpetually seeking that future goal called retirement... and he'd weathered the battering storm as best as he could on his own.

"Okay, Michael," Charlotte urged in an encouraging tone. "Why don't you tell us what happened."

"Tyson punched me," Michael announced succinctly.

Mavis clutched at her scarf, Paul cleared his throat and received a warning glance from Charlotte, and Tyson, unmindful of the instructions, cried out, "I had to make you stop!"

"Tyson," Charlotte said, "you will get your turn. It's Michael's turn now." Her voice remained calm but left no doubt that she meant business. She turned back to Michael. "Can you please give me a little more detail, Michael? Take your time and just tell me what you remember."

"Aren't there recess supervisors?" Mavis demanded. "What kind of school is this that lets my little boy get beat up on the playground?"

Charlotte chose to let the interruption slip by long enough to answer, "We do have supervisors and we care enormously about the safety of the children. But even with the best intentions, we can't see everything that happens.

"But I won't tolerate any more interruptions," Charlotte continued. "If it happens again, I'll ask you to wait outside while I speak to the boys alone. Okay, Michael, please continue."

It was clear that the boy felt very uncomfortable being put on the spot and seemed genuinely bewildered to have found himself in this situation. Despite being wholly on Tyson's side, Paul felt a beat of sympathy for him.

When Michael started talking, all of his

brashness was gone, and he spoke breathlessly as if the blindsiding punch had knocked the wind right out of him.

"I was standing on the playground at recess. I wasn't doing anything. Tyson came up to me and got this real weird look on his face and then he punched me."

"Did you say anything to Tyson before that happened? Or do anything?" Charlotte asked.

"Trying to blame my boy?" Mavis mumbled but stopped herself from continuing before Charlotte had to.

"Uh-uh." Michael shook his head solemnly. "He just punched me. Boom!"

Paul now had a sneaking suspicion that the little boy was starting to enjoy telling his tale.

"Okay, thank you, Michael." It was impossible to tell from Charlotte's demeanor what she was thinking, and that agitated Paul. Not only because of Tyson but also because he didn't like feeling cut off from her.

Charlotte turned to Tyson. "Now I'm going to ask you," she said in the same firm, gentle way, "and I just want you to be honest. Did Michael say or do anything at recess before you punched him?"

"No," Tyson said so quietly they could hardly hear him, but the misery in his voice resounded loud and clear.

Paul leaned forward, on the edge of his chair.

"He didn't *that* time," Tyson continued, "but there were lotsa other times..."

Slowly, the story unfolded: the insults, the constant belittling, but always done in a way that it would be easy to miss—easy for everyone except the victim.

"Mostly he says I'm stupid 'cause I do bad at reading and spelling."

Each of Tyson's words brought a painful jolt of memory to Paul...and a realization of how he had unintentionally hurt his nephew by keeping his secret.

"Okay, then," Charlotte said. "First of all, Tyson and Michael, you're going to start by apologizing to each other. Michael, words like that are very hurtful, but Tyson, hitting someone else is always wrong."

The boys apologized with a lack of sincerity that Paul might have found amusing if he wasn't so devastated.

"And I think I'll have you both stay in at recess for a little while," Charlotte continued. "I feel like you should get to know each other better and show more understanding to each other. Does that sound fair?" She included the adults in her question.

Paul nodded, too overwhelmed to voice his questions and protests.

Mavis said, "I'm not sure. I don't think you've been fair to my boy, but I've got to get to work."

"Please feel free to follow up with me later," Charlotte encouraged.

"I'm satisfied for now with the outcome of this," Mr. Millis said. He glanced at his watch. "I have another meeting. I'll leave you to wrap things up here."

After Mavis and Mr. Millis had left, and the boys had been returned to the classroom, which was being supervised by another teacher, Paul lingered and said, "You know, this is my fault, the trouble Tyson's having."

"What do you mean?" Charlotte asked.

The words felt like inflamed tonsils being scraped out of his throat.

"I can't read."

Charlotte was in shock. She tried to muster all of her professional training to combat that reaction. But warring against her maintaining a professional distance was an almost overwhelming urge to comfort Paul with a hug and words of reassurance…even if she had no idea what those words should be.

Dear Lord, she prayed silently. *I can see that Paul is hurting and has probably been in pain for a long time. Please help me to say*

*and do the right thing, and please be with him
and be a source of comfort to him in whatever way he needs.*

"Do you want to tell me about it?" she
asked. She reached out and touched his hand
softly.

His eyes, edged with shame, met hers. "I'm
not sure that there's much more to say. I can't
read."

"Did the trouble start in school?" Charlotte
prompted gently. "Have you ever been diag-
nosed as being dyslexic? There are ways to
work around that."

"No, nothing like that." Paul spoke sharply
now and sounded almost angry. "I probably
shouldn't have even said anything." He made
as if to leave.

"But you did tell me," Charlotte said. "And
I think it's because you're tired of keeping it
a secret and that you want to be able to help
Tyson as much as you possibly can."

"Please don't tell anyone else!" Paul begged
as he settled back into his chair.

"I won't. I give you my word. I can help
you, Paul—please, if you'll let me. Why do
you think you've struggled with reading?"

"Because—" A fault line of pain split his
voice. "I was bullied so badly in school, it

took everything I had just to survive, let alone learn anything in class."

For one eternal moment, Charlotte wondered if the man beside her was going to be able to continue, but he suddenly sat straighter and gathered himself with all of the courage of someone who had made the best of his life despite bitterly hard circumstances.

Devoid of expression, which somehow made it all the more shattering, Paul told her the story of a little boy who was taunted, ostracized and physically and emotionally bullied for most of his elementary school years. The ache she felt for him filled her bones and stung at the corners of her eyes.

But she couldn't cry. She had to be strong for him.

"When I got to high school," Paul said, "I don't know what happened—maybe they finally got bored of it, or found other things more interesting, but it mostly stopped. I started to work out and I found out I was pretty good at sports and I did well with anything I could use my hands for…"

He stopped talking then and searched her eyes. Charlotte knew that he was looking for judgment or even ridicule. She did her best to convey that what she felt for him was the exact opposite.

"I think I used to have a sense of fairness about life, you know?" Paul said, sounding suddenly exhausted. "You try to be a decent person, do your best, and everything should work out. For the life of me, I couldn't figure out what I'd done to make them hate me so much."

Charlotte was out of her chair almost before she knew it. She put her arms around Paul and pressed her cheek to his hair, which smelled of a pine-scented shampoo.

He stiffened slightly with surprise, then she could feel him hugging her back.

"I'm going to help you, Paul," she said, not allowing him to argue. "I'm going to teach you how to read."

Chapter Fourteen

It took considerable negotiation and promises of discretion, but finally Paul agreed that he would allow Charlotte to help him with his reading. Their game plan was for Charlotte to visit him at his house two or three evenings a week. Tyson would be there and they worried a bit about his questions and what he might think, but it still seemed the best solution in a town where they were bound to be spotted, no matter where they decided to go.

"You can try to teach me," Paul cautioned her. "I really don't know what it's going to accomplish after all this time."

But, despite his protests, Charlotte sensed that it was an enormous relief to Paul to have finally revealed his secret. She was glad that he had chosen to tell her, and that she was in a position to help him.

"It will make such a difference," she insisted. "You're an intelligent man, Paul, otherwise you wouldn't have done as well as you have getting through life, and you're a hard worker and, even more than that, you're a kind, good person. I have every confidence in you."

"Thank you," he said quietly. After a brief silence he asked, "How much will you charge for the tutoring sessions?"

Charlotte blinked. "Charge you? I'm not going to charge you for them! Really, Paul..."

"Well, I'm certainly not going to take up your valuable time for free."

Neither of them was willing to cede to the other. Until Charlotte finally said, "Well... you know, my house still needs some work."

"Done," Paul said. "On one condition."

"Driving a hard bargain, are you?"

"I sure am. I'm more than happy to help you out at your place, but I want you to work alongside me so you gain confidence in yourself to do those kinds of things."

"And I want you to do the same with reading," Charlotte said as an unexpected bubble of happiness grew within her.

"I guess it's a deal then," Paul said.

They shook hands to seal the deal.

It wasn't until Charlotte was home and

checked her cell phone, and saw the messages from her mother and from Bridget, that she wondered what it would take to keep Paul's secret. Meanwhile, she was also waiting to hear back from the missionary program, but for once in her life she hoped the mail would take its time because she still didn't know what answer she wanted to receive.

She returned Bridget's call first because she knew it would be the easier one. Things remained tense between Charlotte and her mother. The doctors couldn't find a physical cause, but her mother's symptoms lingered and worsened—aggravated, Charlotte was sure, by her mother's stress and by her refusing to slow down. But she didn't dare say that to her mother.

Lord, I miss Anna. I miss her all the time. I wish we could talk about her...

She sighed as she dialed Bridget's number.

"Hey!" Bridget answered on the first ring. "I thought I might catch up with you at Seth's today. But I didn't see you there. What were you up to?"

"I had some things to deal with after school," Charlotte replied.

Bridget dropped her voice, as if sharing in a conspiracy. "I wondered about that. I hope everything's okay. The new woman in town—Mavis?—was there getting some take-out coffee and I heard her say a couple of things about her boy and some incident that happened at school. She sounded really upset, Char."

Again Charlotte thought of the time she planned to spend with Paul and the hazards of a small town where precious little went unnoticed.

"Bridge, you know I can't discuss the details of what happened with you."

"I know," Bridget agreed in a cheerfully matter-of-fact way. "But I wanted to give you a heads-up. I don't think you and Mavis are going to be best friends anytime soon."

"That's too bad, because I get the feeling Mavis needs friends."

"I suppose," Bridget said. "Listen, I just wanted to touch base. Supper's at our place on Friday so, if I don't see you on Wednesday night, I'll see you then for sure."

Then Charlotte returned her mother's call. But it was her dad who answered. "Your mom is napping. You might want to try back in a half hour or so."

"I will," Charlotte said. "I love you guys."

"Thank you, Charlotte, that's good to hear."

After they'd hung up, Charlotte still clutched her phone while her thoughts raced. She wished they could find answers for her mother's headaches. She wished that she knew for sure whether or not she really wanted to go away.

Most of all, she wished that Anna was still with them.

They had agreed to start meeting on the first Monday that followed Paul's big revelation. Paul looked around his home, making sure everything was tidy and in place, and that no sticky peanut-butter-and-jelly handprints were going to make an unexpected appearance on walls or countertops.

"Ms. Connelly is coming over *here*?" Tyson asked for the umpteenth time.

Paul remembered the days when it was almost impossible to fathom that teachers actually existed outside the classroom, so he patiently explained again. "Yes, and you're welcome to come and say hello and visit for a few minutes, and then, remember, I said you could watch one episode of that show you like?"

"But staying with you and Ms. Connelly would be more fun."

"I understand that you like Ms. Connelly, Tyson," Paul said. "But we have some…

grown-up stuff to talk about, and I honestly think you'd be bored."

"Does it involve kissing?" Tyson asked with an understanding nod.

"Kissing? What? No!"

The brief but utterly pleasing kiss in front of the school came to Paul's mind, as well as Charlotte's scent of soap and cinnamon toothpaste and her warmth when she hugged him.

"You look kinda flushed, Uncle Paul," Tyson said.

"You'd better scoot and make sure your room is tidy in case Ms. Connelly wants to see it." He hoped that was enough to distract Tyson for the moment. Paul saw the boy's eyes go wide again at the marvel of his teacher coming to his home as he bolted for the stairs.

But his comment had unnerved Paul more than he wanted to admit, even to himself. He had stripped away all of his defenses and showed the rawest part of his pain to Charlotte. But he had done it so he could improve himself and be in a position to help Tyson and to give him the best life possible. He wasn't supposed to still be thinking about how it had felt when she had put her arms around him to comfort him.

While Tyson was upstairs, he hurriedly washed their supper dishes and put them away and surveyed the kitchen with a critical eye.

You have to stop feeling like you're getting ready for a date...

Paul's thoughts were distracted by the sight of Tyson coming jauntily down the stairs. Apparently, he wasn't the only one who thought that Ms. Connelly was worth making an effort for. He was wearing dress pants, a red-and-blue plaid shirt and...

"Tyson...are you wearing a tie?"

The boy stopped at the bottom of the stairs and lifted it up to show it off.

"Yup! It's got snowmen on it."

"I can see that," Paul said. Then he noticed that his nephew's hair looked particularly slick, no cowlicks in sight. He frowned.

"Come here, bud. What's that you've got in your hair?"

"I lotioned it," Tyson said proudly. "I tell ya, it really keeps it in place."

"I imagine it does," Paul said, stifling a laugh. "But, you know, I kind of prefer your natural look. Why don't you go back upstairs and see if you can wash..."

The sound of the doorbell interrupted his instructions.

* * *

Charlotte made a valiant effort not to act surprised when she stepped into Paul's house. She knew that the idea of a bachelor pad was a cliché that didn't suit loyal, hardworking Paul in the least. But while she hadn't expected to see deep maroon furniture and strobe lights, she also hadn't quite expected to see the immaculately groomed yard with its fresh white fence and cluster of cheerful-looking pansies in the earth below the window. She also hadn't been prepared for hardwood floors shined to a gleam, earthy-looking furniture arranged as if people might want to sit down and chat at any time or a butter-yellow kitchen with counter and cupboard space that she couldn't help coveting.

"Wow, you're a lot tidier than I am," she blurted out, despite her best efforts.

"Ah, a closet slob, are we?" Paul said with a droll look.

"Ms. Connelly!" Tyson hurled himself at her and she instinctively reached out her arms to steady him and herself. She was taken aback by the emotions that flooded her for the little boy as she returned his hug. She cared about all of her students, but she couldn't deny that Tyson was starting to hold a special place in her heart…or that his connection to Paul played into that.

God, help me to be balanced and to remember that I'm here to do a job. And please help me to keep my own dreams and goals in mind.

She still hadn't heard back from the mission committee, but she couldn't imagine it would be long now.

Tyson stepped back. "I wore a tie!" he announced proudly.

"I can see that." Charlotte caught Paul's secret smile at her over Ty's head, and again her heart did a two-step. She quickly looked down at Tyson. "The snowmen look very happy."

She registered the overly slick look and lotion-y smell of his hair then and glanced up again at Paul, who shrugged.

"Uncle Paul says you have some grown-up stuff to talk about and that there's no kissing planned," Tyson announced.

"*And* on that note," Paul hurriedly interjected, "this young gentleman was about to go upstairs to try to get some of the lotion out of his hair. As a matter of fact, I should probably give him a hand. Be right back."

He hurried Tyson up the stairs, and Charlotte noticed that he wouldn't look at her. But, frankly, she was glad to have the reprieve. What in the world had that kissing comment been about? Based on experience, she knew that six-year-olds didn't have much of a filter, so she hoped that's all it was. And that Paul didn't think she had hopes for a romance or anything like that.

By the time the two of them returned downstairs, she had composed herself.

"Tyson is going to watch a show in the den while we work," Paul explained. He apparently had decided to deal with the kissing comment by ignoring it. Well, that suited Charlotte just fine.

Tyson's hair was damp and unruly, as she was used to seeing it. His face had that just-scrubbed pink look. He still wore his snowman tie.

"Uncle Paul says that if I'm polite and let you get your work done, I can show you my room before you leave."

"I'd like that very much," Charlotte said.

When Tyson had finally left the room, and it was just the two of them in the kitchen, an expression on Paul's face, somewhere between chagrin and amusement, signaled to Charlotte that he was not as oblivious to Tyson's comment as he was acting.

"Okay, then," she said briskly. "Should we

get started? We might as well use the kitchen table, do you think?"

She thought she saw Paul's eyes shadow a bit as he registered that she was in her teacher mode. She remembered what he had said about there being two different versions of her, and she wondered if he had figured out that it was easier to protect her feelings when she was being professional.

"The kitchen table is fine," he said quietly. He gestured to an empty chair and took one himself. His arms dangled awkwardly at his sides, as if he wasn't quite sure what to do with them.

Charlotte began to busy herself putting picture books and cue cards out on the table, focusing on that so she wouldn't focus on how large and handsome—and yet how vulnerable—Paul looked sitting there.

"Now, with my students, I usually like to start at the beginning," she said, speaking quickly and keeping her attention on the study aids. "Reading begins with the basics—first we start with the letters of the alphabet, we learn their sounds and then we learn how they can be put together to make words. How does that sound?"

There was no answer.

She looked at Paul and saw him looking

back, the half smile on his lips in conflict with the stormy look in his eyes.

"Paul?" she asked nervously. It took effort for her not to fill the silence by repeating what she had just said.

"I think this was a mistake," Paul said.

Chapter Fifteen

The questioning look in Charlotte's violet eyes almost caused Paul to backtrack what he'd said. But he had meant it, and it was important to him that she understood why.

He resisted the urge to take her hands in his as he spoke.

"I am not a six-year-old student," he said, choosing his words carefully. "And I'm not one of the newcomers at church."

"I'm not implying in any way that you're not intelligent," Charlotte interjected. "I already told you how I feel about that."

"Please…just let me continue."

Charlotte opened her mouth, then snapped it shut.

"I don't even know if I can explain this…" Frustrated, he fisted some of his hair in his hand. "It's not that I don't want to learn, but

I don't know if I *can* start at the beginning. I know I have to learn the basics, but I—I really can't stand anything that reminds me of sitting in a classroom. Whatever happened to me, I got through it the best way I could, and I'm living my life the best way I can. I want to do this for Tyson, I do. I just can't do it *this* way."

He watched an array of expressions cross Charlotte's face as he spoke, and he knew she was doing her best to meet him halfway.

"Can I say a couple of things now?" she asked, softly.

He nodded.

"First of all, as I've said before and will say as many times as you need to hear it, you are a good person, Paul Belvedere, and Tyson is blessed to have you as his guardian. No," she stalled his protest, raising her voice slightly. "Now I'm asking you to let *me* finish. The love and care you show Tyson can't be learned from any book, and you've more than proven how capable you are by the way you pay attention and the things you can do and remember."

"So you agree there's no point to this," Paul said, sitting up straighter in his chair and leaning forward.

"No, that's *not* what I'm saying at all."

Charlotte tucked a piece of hair behind her ear. He noticed that she was wearing it down the way he liked it. "What I'm saying is that I think that what you're not admitting is that you don't just want to do this for Tyson. You want to prove something to yourself."

Paul pondered her words, unable or unwilling to know if there was truth in them.

"If we can come up with a way for you to learn that feels comfortable to you," Charlotte said with a thoughtful expression, "would you be willing to try?"

He shifted in his chair in what he knew was a futile attempt to stall for time. Then, in the waiting silence, a delighted chortle came from the den and reminded him that he and Charlotte weren't alone in the house, nor was he alone in this decision.

"I want to do what's best for Tyson." He wasn't ready to concede her earlier point that he himself wanted more. "So if you can think of anything that might help, I'll give it a try. But I can't promise anything beyond that."

Charlotte nodded. "That's good enough for me."

Paul hesitated, uncertain about whether he should bring up what else was on his mind.

"What else are you thinking about?" Charlotte asked, perceptive as always.

He took a deep breath and plunged in. "I'm still thinking about Tyson and what happened at school with Michael. I know you have to be a neutral party," he hurried to assure Charlotte as he saw her posture stiffening. "But I see Ty here at home, and he can be a happy, goofy kid, you know? Like with that tie he's got on and the whole hair-lotion thing."

Charlotte nodded, a smile lifting the corners of her mouth.

"I mean, he still has his moments," Paul continued, "but in general, he's doing a lot better." He shook his head. "I just can't equate the kid who's laughing over some silly show in there with the one who decided the best way to settle his problems was to punch someone."

"We don't always know how people are going to react to things," Charlotte said. "Not children...not even ourselves."

"I suppose not..." Paul shook his head. "It just makes me feel like, wow, did I ever drop the ball on that one. Something I promised myself I'd never do."

"You're only human, Paul. I wonder if you forget that sometimes." Her eyes were soft with understanding. "You're right in saying that I have to stay neutral, but I'm asking you again to trust me and my experience with this. I personally think it will do both Tyson and Michael a lot of good to spend some time together and sort things out, and it will always be under my supervision. You might not want to hear this, but I believe that behind all of that bluster, Michael is just a little boy in pain, too. They may have more in common than you think."

Paul shrugged, again not willing to commit himself. But, once again, Charlotte had made him think. She had a way of challenging him, and although based on his track record, that should have pushed him away, it made him want to get closer to her.

"So…" Charlotte began to gather her training tools back up. "I guess we won't do any more today. Does Ty still want to show me his room before I go, do you think?"

Paul felt bad that she had obviously spent considerable time getting the study materials ready, and before he knew it, the words were out of his mouth. "Why don't you stay and have supper with us?"

The decidedly unprofessional flush on her cheeks made him glad that he had asked.

"That would be nice… I mean, if you're sure."

"Yes, I'd love it if you would stay. I mean,"

Paul hurriedly amended, "*we* would both enjoy the company."

Paul had turned down her offer to help in the kitchen, and Charlotte was secretly relieved. Whenever she was around other couples, it wasn't so much the obvious signs of affection like kisses and embraces that would tug at her. It was things like the intimate dance of familiarity and companionship that she'd observed when couples like Seth and Rena were in their kitchen preparing a meal. She didn't often let herself think about what it would be like to be part of a couple, because life and circumstances just never seemed to point her in that direction. But, if the thoughts came, they were often stirred by the demonstration of a secret language that couples developed over time.

"Ty, now would be a good time to show Ms. Connelly your room," Paul suggested. Tyson was thrilled to oblige, bounding up the stairs while Charlotte followed close behind him.

His room was perfect for a little boy, Charlotte thought, without resorting to the themes of popular comic book and cartoon characters. As she took in the neutral color of the walls, the denim-blue bedspread and the darker blue of the dresser and nightstand, as well as the collection of stuffed toys and small cars that adorned one of the shelves, she again admired Paul for the home he had provided for his nephew. It was obvious to see the care and concern inherent in the surroundings.

But she also noted that there were no books on the shelves and, while she understood why now, she hoped even more fervently that she and Paul could continue to work together and that eventually he would have the basic skills he needed and the confidence to keep building on them.

And she hoped that would all happen before she went away to do her mission work.

"Ms. Connelly?" Tyson looked like he was thinking hard about something, then he gave a firm nod.

"Yes, Tyson?"

"I wanta show you something." He opened the bottom drawer of his nightstand and slid out a picture. He studied it for a moment before handing it to her.

"I don't keep this out all the time because it makes me sad," he said. "But I keep it close so I can look at it when I want to. Uncle Paul says that someday I'll want to have it out all the time."

Charlotte looked at the picture. "I think your uncle Paul is right, Tyson," she said gently. "Thank you so much for sharing this with me."

In the picture, Tyson was sandwiched between his parents, being hugged from both sides, and his mouth was wide-open in a laughing smile. Erica, Paul's sister, had eyes that were hazel, several shades lighter than his dark brown ones, and they were dancing instead of deep and thoughtful, but she had his smile. Tyson's father was boyish looking with red hair and blue eyes, and Charlotte could easily imagine Tyson growing up to look very much like him.

Something his parents would never have the chance to see...

"Ms. Connelly?"

She blinked and did her best to smile at the little boy.

"Yes?"

"Do you think my mom and my dad know that I punched Michael?"

Dear Lord, please help me find the right words.

"I know God knows everything," the little boy continued, "and I axed him to forgive me. But do you think my mom and my dad saw?

Or that God told them about it?" He fixed anxious eyes on Charlotte.

There was so much she could say to Tyson about God and His infinite love, but as an educator she had to tread carefully, especially since she wasn't sure where Paul stood on the matter. It wasn't her place, she knew, but at the same time she couldn't bear to leave Tyson without some kind of answer.

"I think," Charlotte said, "that there's nothing your parents knew or could know about you that would make them stop loving you. You always carry their love right here." She touched her own heart.

Tyson reached out his hand then and she gave the picture back to him. He studied it again before putting it back into the drawer. "My mom used to talk to me about God," he said, "but Uncle Paul doesn't. I don't know if he likes God very much."

"Supper's ready." Paul's voice sounded from just outside the bedroom door, and Charlotte wondered how much he had heard. Still, she was relieved that she didn't have to answer to Tyson's last comment.

Paul felt conflicting emotions swirl around in his head. On the one hand, he was touched that Tyson had chosen to show the picture of his parents to Charlotte—a picture, as it happened, that would turn out to be the last one the three of them would ever take together. He wondered if Charlotte realized the significance of that, because Tyson was very protective of that picture. Sometimes when he went to tuck his nephew in, he would see the little boy hurriedly put it in his drawer and pretend he hadn't been looking at it.

On the other hand, he was feeling guilty. Although he knew he should have made his presence known to his nephew and Charlotte before he had, he couldn't help being curious about how Charlotte would handle Tyson's questions. He thought she had handled herself appropriately, under the circumstances, and with compassion for Tyson. So, in fairness, he knew that the unsettled feeling their conversation had provoked was because of his own feelings. He knew that Erica had expected that he would take Tyson to church and, because of his own struggles with faith, he had failed to do so.

"Uncle Paul makes pretty good mac and cheese," Tyson said. There was no lingering sign of the tough questions he had asked Charlotte. "He says it's one of his spe-shul-tees." He sounded the word out carefully.

Paul could sense that Charlotte was making an effort to catch his eye. He tried to put aside his discomfort and keep his company manners on.

"Where's the blue box?" she asked him over Tyson's head, grinning.

Despite himself, he grinned back. "I'll have you know that this is my own secret recipe."

"Well, in that case, I look forward to eating it."

"There's salad, too," Tyson said. "I sometimes help make it but I was busy showing you my room today. Uncle Paul says that we gotta have our greens. I like ranch dressing best. What do you like?"

"I like ranch, too," Charlotte said.

"Okay, bud, I think Ms. Connelly's probably feeling a little overwhelmed right about now. Although—" he tilted his head at her "—I guess you're probably used to that, with being a teacher and all."

He served Charlotte some of the mac and cheese and passed her the salad and dressing to help herself. Then he served Tyson and himself, and he was about to take a bite when he noticed Charlotte waiting with her hands folded.

He suddenly felt very stubborn.

"Dig in while it's hot," he said, pretending

not to notice that Charlotte was waiting for the food to be blessed.

There was a flicker of hesitation, and then she took a bite.

"It's delicious," she proclaimed, but Paul couldn't help feeling like he had failed another exam.

So, Paul had heard her conversation with Tyson, and now Charlotte couldn't help noticing the point he was making. She knew that not all families prayed before meals, and since she'd never seen them at church for the Sunday service, it wasn't likely they did. But it had become a habit for her, though she certainly hadn't intended to make him feel bad about the omission.

Tyson's oblivious chatter helped smooth things over, and soon Charlotte was eating with even more enjoyment than she had anticipated.

"Admit it," Paul prodded, "you're surprised. Can you taste the secret ingredient?"

"Nutmeg?" Charlotte guessed. "I've heard a lot of people use that to enhance the taste."

"Oh, please, that's for amateurs." Paul rolled his eyes in an exaggerated fashion and she giggled, relieved and happy that they were having fun again.

"Is it your mom's recipe?" she asked.

For a beat she wondered if he was going to answer or if she'd dampened the mood, then he simply said quietly, "Actually, it was Erica's."

She realized Paul must have memorized the recipe. And once again, Charlotte thought how smart he was, with his ability to take in information and retain it.

Tyson had been too busy chasing rogue noodles around with his spoon to pay attention.

"Can I get the ice cream?" he asked.

"You *may*," Paul said, pointedly. "But a polite thing to do is make sure our guest has had enough of the main course first before you offer dessert."

"I have," Charlotte assured them. "It was delicious." She started to get up from her chair. "Can I help clear the table?"

"You're our guest. Don't worry about it, but thanks." Paul said. "Ty, would you please, *very* carefully, take our plates to the kitchen and bring out the ice cream, spoons and bowls? You don't have to do it all in one trip," he cautioned.

"It probably takes three times as long when he helps," Paul remarked when Tyson was in the kitchen. "But I think it's good to let him."

"It's exactly the right thing to do," Charlotte agreed. Then she added in a hurried tone, "Before Tyson's back, I wanted to say that I'm sorry if I offended you. I gather you heard some of our conversation when you came to call us for supper. I want you to know that I'm mindful of boundaries—as a teacher I have to be. But I didn't want to disregard Ty's questions, either, because they're obviously important to him."

"You didn't," Paul said. "Offend me, I mean. Or cross any boundaries."

"Okay, if you're sure. I just sensed something before we started to eat."

"I felt you were waiting for me to say grace," Paul said. "We don't do that."

"So I gathered. It's just what I'm used to. I didn't mean to put any pressure on you."

Paul shifted in his chair. "I'd better go see what's holding Tyson up."

His departure left Charlotte wondering what his thoughts really were on the matter. She hoped she hadn't ruined whatever friendship they had between them; she especially hoped that Paul wouldn't change his mind about getting help with his reading—if she could come up with a way to help that he was comfortable with.

Paul and Tyson returned together, each holding a bucket of ice cream.

"We have mint chocolate chip and cookie dough," Tyson announced excitedly. "What's your favorite? Do you like both? If you can't choose, Uncle Paul will let you have both, but then you get just a little less of each. Still, it's not a bad deal."

"No, it certainly isn't." Charlotte said. "I think I will have both, please."

"Ty, we forgot the toppings!" Paul slapped his palm to his forehead as if he couldn't believe how careless they'd been.

"I'll get them!" Tyson ran back to the kitchen.

"I just felt like we weren't quite done here," Paul said bluntly as soon as his nephew was out of earshot again.

Charlotte waited, remaining silent.

"I feel like I should be apologizing to you," he continued. "You haven't done anything wrong. You've been nothing but kind and helpful to both of us. It's just… I think I've been reminded of something today that I've been trying to avoid thinking about. I know Tyson's parents would have expected me to take him to church and to teach him about faith. But I haven't, because of the struggles I've had with my own faith journey."

"The church would welcome you," Charlotte said. "Just as we've welcomed you on Wednesday nights."

"What about God?" Paul asked, searching her eyes. "What does He think of all of this?"

"He welcomes you…" Charlotte's cell phone began to ring. "It's Rena," she said, puzzled. "Excuse me, but I'd better take this. Hello, Rena?"

"Where are you?" Rena asked.

"Why are you looking for me?" Charlotte said, avoiding the question of where she was. Then she swallowed panic as she asked, "Is it my mother? Did something happen? Is she all right?"

"No," Rena said. "It's Mrs. Cannon—Michael's mom. She came into the café and demanded to know if I'd seen you. I tried to encourage her to make an appointment with you at the school, but she was upset and causing a bit of a scene, so I took her phone number and I promised her I'd pass it on to you. I'm worried, Charlotte. She's definitely on the rampage."

Chapter Sixteen

"Ms. Connelly is very nice," Tyson said as Paul tucked him in that night.

"Yes, she is," Paul agreed.

"She saw my room."

"She did, and she liked it."

Tyson wriggled around in bed, getting his head into exactly the right spot on the pillow. He sighed and closed his eyes.

Then for some reason, his nephew's eyes flew open again.

"She likes the same kind of ice cream as me, *both* kinds."

"Uh-huh," Paul said.

"You should marry her," Tyson proclaimed.

Paul wanted to laugh it off, but something in the innocent suggestion got under his skin. He realized that something had been nudging at him ever since he had overheard their conversation before supper. It wasn't just the fact that they'd been talking about God and church and Tyson's parents; it was that Tyson was talking to Charlotte in a way that he never talked to him. And he wondered what it might be like to have someone in his life who cared for Tyson, too, and who could help him answer the hard questions.

But he couldn't drag Charlotte—or anyone else—into his world. He had too many emotional scars and too many limitations. She'd stay in his life strictly on a professional basis. In fact, come next June, she wouldn't be in his life at all. He had to keep that in mind and protect himself from getting too close.

Even if he couldn't stop thinking about the way her eyes danced when she teased him about macaroni and cheese.

But then she'd received that phone call and, even though she'd assured him that everything was fine and had made a big show of enjoying her ice cream, he knew that something had happened, something that she wasn't willing to share.

"Uncle Paul?" Tyson's drowsy voice pulled Paul away from his thoughts.

"Yeah, bud? You know it's time for you to go to sleep."

"I know," Tyson said around a yawn. "I just

wanted to tell you that I showed Ms. Connelly my picture. You know…?"

"Yes," Paul said gently. "I know what picture you mean."

"Is that okay, Uncle Paul?"

Ah, so now there was this question to add another ingredient to the bittersweet mix.

"Of course it's okay, Ty. If you felt like it was the right thing to do, then it was the right thing to do."

Tyson sighed and nodded, then flipped over onto his stomach. "Will you draw pictures on my back until I go to sleep?"

"I'll stay for five minutes," Paul compromised.

Tyson closed his eyes, but before a slower, deeper breathing could signal that he was asleep, Paul found himself with his own question.

"Tyson…would you…would you like to go to church on Sunday?"

He felt the little boy's back go taut under his hand.

"For real?" Tyson asked.

"Yes, if you'd like."

"Yay!" After the brief exclamation, the little boy closed his eyes again, and just before he drifted off, he mumbled, "Mom'll be so glad…"

* * *

Charlotte decided to take the proactive approach in dealing with Mavis and whatever her concerns were. She had no desire to avoid her and, even if she had, it was foolish to think she could do so in a place the size of Green Valley. She didn't intend to avoid Seth's Café, or the grocery store, or anywhere else.

The problem was, now she couldn't track Mavis down. When she called the phone number that Rena had provided for her, the message kept telling her that the customer was out of the service area. It also appeared that Mavis didn't have any trouble avoiding the typically frequented places.

Charlotte thought about asking Michael how she could get hold of his mother, but she immediately dismissed the idea. She wasn't a fan of involving children in adult problems. But she wished she could find out where Mavis was and what was on her mind—although she felt like she had a pretty good idea.

But, in the midst of all of it, the blessing was that Tyson and Michael were actually getting along okay. They weren't exactly best friends—far from it—but after the first day, a kind of silent acceptance seemed to have sprung up between them, one that Charlotte hoped could eventually develop into friendship. The problem with spending recesses supervising a silent classroom was that it gave her far too much time to think about things: about Mavis…and about Paul.

And then there was the question of her overseas missionary work. A letter had arrived for her yesterday. She hadn't opened it yet.

Her heart told her that she already knew the reason why. She just wasn't willing to listen yet.

On Sunday morning, Tyson hopped three times on one foot, three times on the other, then spun in a circle with his arms spread wide. "Ready to go, Uncle Paul?"

"Almost," Paul said, feeling considerably less excited than his nephew for their Sunday morning venture. He was particularly apprehensive about being swarmed by curious people. Even if they were well-meaning, he just hated it when people made a big deal out of someone coming back after a long absence, or someone showing up who had never been there before. He reminded himself that many of these people were the same ones he saw on Wednesday nights.

Charlotte would be there, he had no doubt of that. He couldn't help imagining her face when she saw them. Would it light up with pleasure? He felt pleased at the thought of her being happy to see them.

But he wasn't doing this for her—he was doing it for Tyson.

"Stop with the spinning, please," he said to Tyson, his nervousness making him less patient than usual. "You're going to knock something over."

Tyson stopped but continued to bounce on his heels like they had springs in them. He was particularly excited to see Max at Sunday school. He had on his good dress pants and a button-down shirt and his hair was behaving, but Paul didn't expect that would last for long.

As for himself, he felt completely stiff in his good clothes, like his broad shoulders were going to split the seams of his dress shirt. Maybe it was because he only dressed up for special occasions like weddings…and funerals.

I'm doing this for Tyson and for you and Ross, Erica. Can you ask that God you believe in so much to help me out here?

The church was humming with people when they stepped in. Tyson spotted Max almost immediately and ran off to greet her, leaving Paul to his own devices. Without meaning to, he found his eyes sweeping the room for Charlotte. He felt a combination of anticipation and nervousness knowing that if she was there, she would be with her family. He'd already sensed that they weren't his type…or, rather, that he wasn't theirs. Which made him all the more curious about the strong attachment he felt to their daughter.

"Paul? Is that you?" Ralph Meyer came toward him. The older man was wearing a suit, but with his ramrod posture, closely cropped hair and perpetually watchful expression, he would always look like a police officer no matter how many years he was retired.

Just as Paul was preparing to answer him, Ralph said in his blunt way, "Good, you're here. One of the legs keeps buckling on the Sunday school craft table. We should have time to have a look at it before the service starts."

Lord, You have a funny way of answering prayers, Paul thought, in what felt like the first real communication with God he'd attempted in years. He hadn't expected to be casually put to work on the first Sunday he'd come back to church but, at the same time, it did help ease the path. He left Tyson with Eugenie, the high school student who worked at Seth's Café, then followed Ralph downstairs to the Sunday school rooms.

When he saw the rooms that had been set up with obvious amounts of care and creativity, he could picture Tyson's joy at being there and choosing from the many activities to participate in, and he was happy that they had come.

"Does Charlotte Connelly ever teach Sunday school?" Paul blurted out, wondering where that had come from.

At Ralph's probing look—*once a police officer, always a police officer*—Paul quickly amended. "Ms. Connelly, I mean…she's my nephew's teacher at school, so I just wondered…"

"I believe she might fill in from time to time," Ralph said, his tone as dry as autumn tree bark. "If there's a real need for it. But her regular gig teaching school keeps her busy enough and, of course, she's been helping you out on Wednesday nights."

Ralph's expression, like he was waiting for Paul to fill in the blanks, caused Paul to change the subject.

"Which table leg is wobbly?" he asked.

By the time they got back upstairs, the opening hymn was in progress and Paul went up a side aisle, searching for an empty seat.

His preference would have been the back row, but it was filled with slightly beleaguered-looking parents with infants. So he slid into a row a bit farther up and avoided looking around to see who was near him and who had noticed his entrance. He picked up the bulletin that the usher had pushed into his hand with a quick nod of greeting as he hurried in, and pretended to study it.

Once the service started, Paul found, to his surprise, that it was a little like putting on an old garment that he hadn't worn in years, but that brought a kind of comfort with it. The pastor's sermon on forgiveness contained a line that Paul knew he wouldn't be able to shake away: "Sometimes the hardest person to forgive is yourself."

When they stood to sing "Amazing Grace," the words that had been buried somewhere within his heart found their way to his mouth and poured out. He recalled that, as a youth, he had been told he had a good singing voice and urged to join the choir. But, in those days, he'd viewed everything as an opportunity for others to bully him, so he hadn't joined.

Then a joyfully soaring soprano behind him captured his attention and made it impossible, at least for the moment, to be anything but hopeful. He couldn't help himself.

He turned his head to see who that uplifting sound was coming from and found himself looking into Charlotte Connelly's violet eyes.

Charlotte had seen Paul come in, but she had also seen his need for invisibility, so she had given him his space. When he turned around and saw that she was right behind him, his eyes widened with surprise, and with something else, but he turned back toward the front before she could quite decipher what that something was.

When the service ended, it was her turn to be surprised when he turned again to speak to her instead of bolting toward the nearest exit.

"That's some voice you've got," he said.

She blushed. "Thank you. I love to sing, especially those songs that just speak right to your heart, you know? You're not so bad yourself."

The tips of Paul's ears actually turned red. The sight of a strong, handsome man blushing did things to Charlotte's emotions that she knew she should probably ignore. One of these days she truly did have to sit down with God and sort out what she was supposed to do with her life…and whether Paul Belvedere was meant to be part of it in any serious way. She just hoped she was willing to accept whatever direction the Lord planned to lead her in, even if that meant her being led away from Paul.

"Are you going to introduce us to your friend, Charlotte?" Her mother's voice immediately pulled Charlotte away from her fanciful thoughts.

"This is Paul Belvedere," she said. "He's the uncle of one of my students. Paul, these are my parents, George and Lenore Connelly."

They shook hands and exchanged pleasantries, although Charlotte could only imagine that Paul must be itching to bolt. Of course her parents knew who he was, because of what had happened to his sister, if nothing else. But clearly her mother wanted to know what his role was in Charlotte's life.

"What did you think of the sermon?" Lenore asked Paul. "I hope that we'll be seeing you here more often?"

"It was an excellent sermon," Paul answered, but he didn't respond to the second part of the question. Paul darted a single, pleading look in Charlotte's direction.

"I guess Tyson must be waiting for you to pick him up," she said. "Come on, I'll help you track him down. I'll talk to you later, Mom and Dad. Enjoy your Sunday afternoon."

Before they could say anything else, she headed out of her row. Paul did the same in his and they met in the aisle.

"If we go this way, we'll be able to skip the meet and greet," she said bluntly. Then as they headed toward the Sunday school rooms, she softened as she realized what it must have taken for Paul to show up, and said, "I'm so glad you came. So…what did you think?"

"I only did it for Tyson," he said, avoiding her gaze.

"Oh. Well, of course…"

"But," Paul conceded, looking back at her, "I liked it more than I thought I would. It felt… I don't know. I guess it felt more familiar than I thought it would."

"God always remembers us even when we've been ignoring Him for a long time," Charlotte said quietly. "And He has His ways of drawing us back."

For a moment Paul looked like he was going to agree, or at least be willing to be drawn into a deeper conversation, but then it was like a blind had been drawn down over his face, shutting out the light.

"I'm sure being here on Wednesday nights has a lot to do with it feeling familiar, too," he said.

Charlotte told herself not to be disappointed or to expect too much. It was a huge step that Paul had come to Sunday service at all. She knew that people never responded well to being pushed toward God, especially if they had once known Him but had felt their faith had been betrayed. Knowing what she did now about Paul's experiences with bullying, she couldn't honestly blame him for his feelings. It was almost impossible not to ask where God was when horrible things happened. Some people clung more tightly to God in those times, as she had; some, like Paul, shoved Him away.

"Speaking of Wednesday nights…" She glanced around and lowered her voice. "It still baffles me how you can do such a great job of teaching when…"

Paul shifted from one foot to the other, looking very uncomfortable.

"Tyson should be out of Sunday school soon, shouldn't he?" he interjected.

"He'll be fine with Eugenie until you pick him up. The kids like to stay and play as long as they can. Please, Paul, I really want to know. It might help me figure out how I can help you."

"I'm not even sure I can explain it…" Something in his eyes deepened, and his hands instinctively made gestures like he was holding something. "Whenever I pick up a tool, or work on a car engine, it's like…it's like I have the memories of them in my hands and I just know what to do." His mouth lifted in a rueful smile. "Even if I couldn't look up the names of any of the tools if I had to."

"I have an idea…" Charlotte said as something started to take shape in her mind. "A way to help you learn to read that I think will mean something to you. But, Paul, we have to start with the basics—the ABCs—there's no getting around that."

Paul shook his head, not saying no, she knew, but in an expression of frustration. Charlotte didn't know exactly how, but she felt like she knew this man's heart and knew how important it was to him to feel accepted and to have honor and purpose in his life.

"I'll tell you what," she said. "Next time you come over to help me with a project, I'll write down the names of everything we use and you can see what the words look like, at the same time as you're holding the tools and using them. That way, you can connect the words with things you already know and…" She stopped speaking abruptly as something…

She saw Paul register her expression and

turn to look. He turned back to her with a grim expression.

Across the room, Mavis stood holding Michael's hand. Her eyes met Charlotte's with a mixture of ferocity and fear. A bruise the color of a spoiling plum marred one cheek.

"I have to go," Charlotte said hurriedly.

Chapter Seventeen

"I liked Sunday school a lot," Tyson said while eating a grilled cheese sandwich after church.

"Swallow before you talk, bud," Paul cautioned, then added, "That's good, I'm glad."

"I liked it so much I want to be there all the time."

Apparently, his nephew didn't believe in subtlety. "We'll see what we can do."

"Did you like it too, Uncle Paul?" Tyson persisted. "Church, I mean."

Paul stirred the chicken rice soup that was simmering on the stove and tried to focus his thoughts. Unbeknownst to the little boy, his simple question didn't have a simple answer—especially when he was mulling over Charlotte's proposal for teaching him and still trying to process her unceremonious departure.

He had stayed long enough to watch her approach Mavis and Michael before he turned away and went to get Tyson from the Sunday school room. He knew why she would approach them—that was just Charlotte— and while her kindness and inclusive nature was a big part of what drew him to her, he couldn't deny how disgruntled he felt seeing her talk to them.

"Uncle Paul, did you like church? Is the soup almost ready?"

"Yes, sorry, Ty. I guess I'm daydreaming." He spooned soup into a bowl and then opened the freezer to get an ice cube to cool it more quickly for Tyson. "I did like church. I liked the songs, and the pastor had some good things to say."

Tyson gave a sigh of deep contentment. "I knew you'd like it if you just gave it a chance."

Paul knew there was no way he could explain to a six-year-old how deeply conflicted his feelings really were on the matter, but for the time being, it was enough for him to know that he had made Tyson happy.

He let his nephew's happy chatter and innocuous questions wash over him, giving him reprieve from the place where his mind—and heart—kept wanting to go.

He was beginning to hope that Charlotte

Connelly's concern for him meant that he was important to her, and not just because it was her nature. But seeing how instinctively she responded to Mavis and Michael had him rethinking things. Besides, wasn't it better to detach himself now before he was forced to at the time of her departure?

His phone rang, and he made a futile effort not to hope that it was her.

"Paul? Harold, here," his boss said. "Listen, I'm sorry to bother you on a Sunday, but I need you to open the shop tomorrow. My tooth flared up again and I've got an early appointment with the dentist."

"Sure, I'll be happy to do that," Paul said.

"Thanks. Oh, and I think that new woman in town—Mavis?—will be stopping by with her car. I saw her at church today and she says she needs some work done on it as soon as possible. I don't know what that's all about but I couldn't help but feel bad for her, you know? She looks pretty rough and I can only imagine why. Anyway, I told her we'd squeeze her in if you can manage."

Paul hesitated as thoughts raced through his mind.

"Paul?" Harold's questioning voice came over the line. "Is that okay with you?"

"It's fine," he said. "Thanks for letting me

know." He hung up the phone and tamped down his displeasure before turning his attention back to Tyson.

"Have you had enough to eat? What would you like to do now?"

"I dunno…" The boy shrugged, then his face lit up with an idea. "Can Ms. Connelly come over again?"

Maybe it would be easier to battle his own attachment to Charlotte if his nephew wasn't so clearly attached, too.

Charlotte tried to enjoy the leftover chili she was having for lunch but had no appetite for it. As soon as she had headed in Mavis's direction, the other woman had grabbed her son's hand and they had hurriedly gone in another direction, which puzzled Charlotte because the message she had received was that Mavis was insistent on talking to her. So, why was she avoiding a perfectly good opportunity to do so, and if she wanted to avoid people, what had brought her to church in the first place?

Her phone rang, interrupting her speculations.

"Hello?" she answered.

"You and Paul rushed off in church today,"

her mother said. "It would have been nice to get to know him a little better."

"I'm sorry about that," Charlotte said. "But his nephew was waiting to be picked up." She didn't add that she also had no desire to have them make more of her friendship with Paul than it was, especially since it would make her decision whether to leave or not even more difficult if she longed for more.

"Still…if he's in your life…" her mother prompted.

"He's not," Charlotte answered quickly. "Like I told you, we're just friends. His nephew is in my class." She changed the subject then by asking how her mother was feeling.

"Unfortunately, not well, and those doctors still aren't giving me any satisfactory answers."

After promising to pray for her mother's improved health and an assurance that of course she would be at family dinner on Friday night, Charlotte ended the call.

She sat without moving for a moment, still holding her phone, then set it down and went to find the unopened letter about her missionary work application. She held it in her hands, feeling like the paper weighed more than it possibly could. She didn't know why she was so hesitant to see what the answer was. She wanted to leave everything that was tying her down here, didn't she?

But then Paul Belvedere's face came into her mind, and she asked herself if living life for her own goals alone was truly what she wanted to do. Because she realized that each time she tried to convince others that there was nothing between them other than their connection through Tyson and their Wednesday night activities, she was also trying to convince herself. But she didn't want to fall into the trap of wanting something that wasn't meant to be. Paul had his own priorities, which included keeping up an emotional wall that wouldn't completely let anyone in. She understood why, but it didn't mean she wanted to open herself up for rejection.

No, the answer was to stay focused on her own goals. She went over to the kitchen drawer that held miscellaneous items and rummaged in it to retrieve a letter opener. When she opened the letter, she read:

Dear Ms. Connelly,
We were so pleased to receive your application that expressed your interest in volunteering with our program. Therefore, we are especially pleased to tell you

that we believe that you are a perfect fit, so please consider this your invitation to join us…

Charlotte scanned over the rest of the letter, which talked about the importance of making sure that her passport was valid and that her vaccinations were up-to-date. It then went on to give a briefing of the political climate of the countries she could be sent to and reminded her of the importance of discretion, both for her own safety and the safety of those she would be helping.

Charlotte set the letter aside and waited for something in her heart to tell her that God had answered her prayer, some feeling of happiness or at least of reassurance to come over her, but her feelings were ambivalent.

She retrieved her phone and spontaneously made a call before she could talk herself out of it.

"Paul? It's Charlotte. I hope I didn't catch you at a busy time. Sorry I had to take off so suddenly at church today. I was wondering when we could get together to do some work around my house and try out that teaching idea I had."

She could hear his slight intake of breath that signified someone being caught off guard, and she hoped that she hadn't overstepped her boundaries. But then Paul spoke, and she was warmed by his surprised but not displeased tone.

"I wasn't expecting to talk to you again today," he said. "Ty and I just finished lunch not that long ago."

"I've finished lunch, too," she told him, not bothering to mention her lack of appetite for it.

And definitely not telling him that she had been accepted to the missionary work program.

"This is a coincidence," Paul said. "Tyson was just asking about you."

"Is that Ms. Connelly?" Charlotte could hear Tyson faintly in the background and she smiled.

"Tell Tyson I said hello."

"I will, but right now he's supposed to be rinsing off his dishes," Paul said. "Not eavesdropping on my phone calls."

Their shared laughter made Charlotte feel bonded to him. She rarely allowed herself to imagine what it might be like to be married and to have children that she and her husband could rejoice and fret over, and teach by example how to love and be loved. Until quite recently, she had believed that her role in life was to try to make up for loss, to try to fill in gaps wherever they were and in whatever way she could. And even when she had been struck by the almost unbearable need to escape her family's expectations, she still hadn't thought of allowing the simple dreams of her heart to blossom.

So why did the sudden picture in her mind of Paul and Tyson and her together rock her with such sharp, sudden emotion that she wanted to laugh and cry at the same time?

Don't go there, she cautioned herself. It wouldn't be fair to either of them, and it wouldn't be fair to a little boy who had already lost more than any child should have to endure when she went away. Because she would go away, she told herself firmly. She couldn't let herself down.

"You said you had some projects you need help with?" Paul's question brought her focus back to the phone conversation.

"Yes."

"I'm happy to help," Paul said in a cautious voice, "But I don't need 'make busy' work because you're making *me* into some kind of project."

"No, I really could use your help," Charlotte assured him. "It just makes sense to me that we can help each other at the same time.

Like I mentioned, you do have to commit to learning the basics because you won't get anywhere without them, but I was hoping to help you put the basics together, sounding things out, knowing what letters make what sounds and that kind of thing, using the things that interest you and that you work with every day. What do you think?"

The silence on the other end of the phone didn't unnerve her. She could visualize the intent expression that Paul got when he was thinking something through.

"What about Tyson?" he asked. "I mean, I can see how something like that would help me with the class on Wednesday nights and with my job, and that's all great. But the only real reason I'm doing this is for Tyson, and if I can't help him with the things he's going to need help with, what good is it?"

"Because once you start to learn," Charlotte hurried to reassure him, "you'll begin to discover that there are patterns to words and to reading that are applicable in all cases. I really think this could work. Are you willing to give it a try?"

"I…guess it wouldn't hurt to try," Paul said slowly. "Maybe we could pop by tomorrow night?"

"That should be fine." Charlotte quelled

the pleasure that wanted to tap-dance through her. It wasn't a date; it was an opportunity to help one another.

"By the way," Paul said, a note of humor coming into his tone, "whatever projects you've got planned, I don't intend to do them for you, but I'm happy to supervise while you do them."

"Excuse me?" Charlotte said, matching his bantering tone.

"Don't you want to prove that you picked up at least some skills on Wednesday nights? I need proof that I'm right when I think we make a great team."

The statement hung between them for a moment and, even though Charlotte knew they were joking around, it felt heavy with implications.

"No answer to that?" Paul prodded gently. "You know I'm just giving you a hard time, right?"

"I know." She made herself laugh. "So you and Tyson will come by tomorrow?"

"Yes. I'll let you know if anything changes. Speaking of Tyson, there's a certain someone here who knows who I'm talking to and is bouncing off the walls. I'd better get going."

"Okay," she said.

"Before I go," Paul said, "did you, um, catch up with Mavis?"

She could hear his effort to make it sound like a casual question, but he didn't quite pull it off.

"No, I didn't," she answered. She didn't add any further details because there was no point in doing so. She knew he would feel better if she had little or nothing to do with them, and she couldn't abide by that. It was her job. Michael was her student, too.

"I hope you watch yourself around them," Paul said darkly. "I don't trust either of them."

Charlotte knew that he hadn't noticed the signs of domestic abuse on Mavis's face. It wasn't her place to mention it, but surely he would have empathy for Mavis if he knew.

"I think," she said, choosing her words carefully, "there is usually more to people than we first realize, and that everyone has reasons for doing what they do, even if they keep those reasons hidden."

As she said the words, she thought about Anna and how Paul didn't even know that she used to have a sister. Despite the town's tendency to get involved and share news, she knew that, out of respect for her family and because of the dreadful circumstances of it all, there wasn't anyone who would tell Paul.

They would leave it up to her whether or not she wanted to share what happened. She wondered if she did, whether it would strengthen their bond of friendship or if he would feel like it was another of the many betrayals in his life that she hadn't told him sooner.

"I suppose," Paul said, sounding thoughtful. "Anyway, I really better go now. Hope to see you tomorrow."

"Yes, tomorrow," Charlotte echoed, her heart singing as she hung up the phone.

Chapter Eighteen

Paul walked Tyson to school on Monday morning. Since his conversation with Charlotte was still on his mind, before he dropped him off, he asked Tyson, "How's it going with Michael? Be honest."

"It's pretty good," Tyson said cheerfully.

"Are you sure?"

"Yeah, it's good. He likes turtles, too."

"Oh? Well…that's great. You know I just want you to be safe and happy, right, bud?"

"Sure, Uncle Paul, I know. You tell me that all the time."

As he continued on to Harold's, Paul thought he would have to give Charlotte her due for getting positive results out of the situation. Although he still struggled with trusting that it wasn't just the calm before another storm. He still worried about dealing with

Mavis that morning at the shop. He wished that he'd been able to tell Charlotte about the appointment and how he felt about it, but she had made that comment about there always being a reason behind the way people acted, and it had touched a nerve. She had a way of doing that—of challenging his perception of things—and perhaps the thing that unsettled him the most was that he knew how readily he had come to rely on that.

She made him want to be more than who he was.

He had hoped to have time to gather himself before the appointment, but Mavis was sitting outside the shop in her car, one that would be referred to as a clunker. She was obviously anxious to get things done.

He caught her eye through the car window and gave her a terse wave, then signaled "two minutes" with his fingers. The woman, nodded, unsmiling, and it struck him that she would be no more thrilled to face him than he was to deal with her—she was only doing so out of sheer necessity.

Inside the shop he took a deep breath and tried to calm and prepare himself with something that felt uncannily like prayer. *So, God, I haven't forgotten how to talk to You...*

I just didn't want to remember why I needed to do it...

When he unlocked the door for Mavis, he still wasn't looking forward to it, but he felt the certainty that he could deal with it. Whatever her attitude, he promised himself that he would be professional, calm and tactful. He wanted to be the kind of person who Charlotte would be proud of, but pressing even more on his heart at the moment was that he wanted to be the kind of person who *God* could be proud of.

Mavis stepped into the shop, and Paul immediately noticed that she was wearing sunglasses. But then something in Mavis's careful, self-conscious body language and the angle she held her head at signaled to him that she was hiding something—not in a malicious way, but in way that he all too readily recognized.

It's none of your business, he tried to tell himself. But immediately a thought battered at him: *There were too many people minding their own business when they could have been helping you.*

"Are you all right?" he asked before he could talk himself out of it.

"What do you mean?" He could sense Mavis putting up an invisible shield.

God...? I'm out of practice with this prayer business, but I think You know I need help here.

The answer that came into his heart was *Do unto others*. No matter what his feelings were about Mavis and no matter what his worries were about Tyson and Michael, he knew that he couldn't allow himself to ignore what he suspected.

"Are you...are you hurt?"

"Hurt? What are you talking about?" She threw the words back at him, attempting to make a mockery of his question.

But he recognized the caved-in shoulders, the retreating into oneself with such acuity, he could feel the answering memory of his own body language.

When he'd started high school, he'd found himself in a sea of new, uncertain students, not doted over but finally no longer bullied, although the inner scars would remain. It had taken him almost a year to learn how to stand up straight again.

In grade ten, he'd hit a growth spurt, found a natural affinity for running and made the track team. He was suddenly accepted, even popular, but he never forgot his past, and he'd kept his heart hidden from everyone. Including his family.

Then Charlotte Connelly had come along, and he found his heart heading into dangerous territory.

"Do you need help?" he asked Mavis. "Someone to talk to?"

"Of course not!" she snapped at him. "I came in here to get my car looked at, not to get psychoanalyzed or whatever it is you're trying to do. In fact, I'm finding your attitude very inappropriate. Where's your boss?"

"Harold had an appointment this morning. I'm very sorry, I meant no disrespect. Will you let me have a look at your car?"

Her posture and expression showed that she was in a battle with herself. No doubt she wanted nothing more than to bolt out the door, but her car needed fixing and there was nowhere else she could go unless she wanted to risk driving it into Regina. Finally she turned back to him and, sounding like she felt disgusted with herself for her own weakness, said, "I think it's the battery." Then she suddenly burst into bone-shaking sobs.

Paul hurried her into the office in back, grabbing a handful of tissues out of a box on the way.

It was amazing that no matter how long it had been since he'd done so, when there was a crisis, praying for guidance felt surprisingly natural.

He ushered Mavis to sit down and handed her some tissues, which she balled into her fists, unmindful of the tears streaming down her cheeks.

Paul sat down in the chair across from her and didn't say anything, just let her cry, willing to wait for as long as she needed. When she finally made the snuffling, hiccupping sounds that signaled the end of a cry, he handed her a clean batch of tissue and said, "Please tell me what I can do to help. I really do want to help."

It had been a particularly busy day at school, and the students were more rambunctious than usual for some reason.

Paul had left a cryptic message on Charlotte's phone. "Call me as soon as you can. I need to talk to you about Mavis... How does Michael seem? Never mind—I'll talk to you when you phone me."

She simply hadn't found a minute to spare, and she hoped Paul didn't think she was purposely ignoring his call.

As Charlotte ate her chicken salad sandwich during her lunch break, she considered popping in on Paul at the garage. But just as she had swallowed her last bite, taken a sip from her water bottle and reached for her purse, her phone rang, and the call display showed that it was Bridget.

"Hi, Bridge, What's up?"

"I should be asking you that." Her cousin's voice came over the phone petulantly. "I feel like we never get a chance to talk these days."

"I see you at family dinner every week," Charlotte reminded her.

"That's not what I mean," Bridget said. "We don't really talk there—we listen to our parents talk."

Charlotte realized then that Bridget sounded genuinely upset and wasn't just vying for attention.

"I just finished lunch and was thinking about taking a walk," she said. "Are you free right now? We could meet up?"

"Seth's in five?"

"I'll see you there."

Charlotte ended the call and sighed. *Okay, God, I get it.* It seemed like she was being perpetually reminded that she wasn't in the place in her life where she could pursue whatever it was that might be worth pursuing with Paul. Someone in her family always needed her for one reason or another, and if she begrudged them that, then didn't that make her a horrible person? Especially when there wasn't any way she could possibly make up for what happened to Anna.

She slung her purse over her shoulder and headed toward Seth's Café, trying her best not to think about Paul's earlier call. She promised herself that she would phone him back when she could, but she couldn't leave Bridget feeling neglected, either.

Soon, she sat across from her cousin at a corner table in Seth's. Seth himself stopped by their table shortly after they arrived.

"Are you here for lunch, ladies?" he asked, grinning widely. "I have some beef stew that would hit the spot on a day like this."

"Just coffee for me, thanks, Seth," said Charlotte.

"I'll have coffee, too," Bridget said. "Sorry, Seth, I'm just not that hungry."

"No worries," Seth said cheerfully, filling their mugs with the pot he carried. "Charlotte, if you see my lovely wife this afternoon," he added, "could you remind her that we have choir practice tonight?"

"I sure will."

As soon as Seth departed, Charlotte asked, "Okay, Bridge, what's the matter?"

Bridget looked for a moment like she was going to deny that anything was wrong, but then she shrugged her shoulders and said, "I'm not exactly sure. I've just been feeling out of sorts. There's nothing wrong that I can put my finger on, but things don't feel exactly right, either."

"I wonder if that's just life," Charlotte said, thoughtfully. "I mean, I hate to say this, but maybe it's only when we're really young that we believe that we'll suddenly have everything figured out when we're grown-up. Maybe life—and faith—isn't anything more than just seeing what each day brings and doing our best with it."

"Not helping, Char," Bridget said in such an exasperated tone that Charlotte couldn't help chuckling.

"I'm at a bit of a loss," she admitted. "I count on you to be the dreamer, Bridge. I'm the responsible one, remember?"

Bridget attempted a smile, but it fell flat.

"Please talk to me," Charlotte insisted, feeling a sudden stab of apprehension.

"I don't know, Char… I just feel like you're drifting away from us. Even if you don't go overseas, I can see how interested you are in Paul Belvedere, whether you want to see it yourself or not, and I can see how important he and Tyson have become to you. Maybe I do just wish things could have stayed the way they were when we were kids and everything seemed so carefree."

"Bridget?" Charlotte swallowed an emotional surge. "Do you…ever think…about Anna?"

Something hard and flinty came into Bridget's eyes. "Let's not talk about her."

"But, Bridge…"

"Please."

Bridget picked up her mug and took another swallow of her coffee.

"I guess I've kind of messed up your lunch break," she said as she set her coffee back down again.

"No, it's okay," Charlotte said, though she was feeling troubled by what Bridget had said—and by what she had refused to say. "But I guess I should be getting back. Bridge, you know that family means everything in the world to me, right?"

"I do. I know we're important to you. But that doesn't mean that you don't want other things—other people—in your life."

"But so do you, Bridge," Charlotte pointed out. "You might be going through a bit of a rough patch right now, but I know you hope to meet someone who's right for you. Maybe… maybe I just want the same."

And what's wrong with that, Charlotte

thought as she walked back to the school, unsure of whether she was asking the question of herself or of God. But the anguishing perpetual question of whether she could please others and still be happy herself remained unanswered.

Then her phone rang, showing Paul's number again. She might not have the answers she was looking for but she wasn't going to keep him waiting any longer.

"Paul? Hi. Yes, I got your messages—it was a very hectic morning, and then I used what I had left of my lunch break to meet up with Bridget. She's going through kind of a tough time. You said you wanted to talk to me about Mavis?"

"It's okay," Paul said, and she heard relief in his voice. "Listen, I know you have to get back to class, but you're still expecting Tyson and me at your place tonight, right?"

A small butterfly of anticipation fluttered through her, one that she quickly netted.

"We can talk then," she said. "But remember that we've got other work to do." She was reminding herself as much as Paul.

"I know," he said. "But I wouldn't feel right if I didn't tell you. Mavis needs help."

Chapter Nineteen

"Is this where you live?" Tyson asked, awe-struck, as he and Paul stepped into Charlotte's house.

"It sure is," Charlotte replied, smiling at Paul over the boy's head in a way that did unfamiliar but not unpleasant things to his heart.

He loved the way Charlotte's house was full of the same appealing contradictions as she was, with its warm colors and collection of furniture, pictures and knickknacks, each one chosen, as she'd explained to him, because it appealed to something in her and not because it matched a particular decorating scheme. It reminded him again how intriguing he found the different facets of her personality.

I could spend the rest of my life getting to know this woman.

Where had that thought come from? He liked Charlotte and he no longer bothered denying to himself that he was attracted to her. But there was no happily-ever-after in the works here—not with her intentions to go overseas. Somehow, he managed to keep forgetting that.

Charlotte ushered them in and beckoned them to take off their coats, which she hung on a coatrack that was tan with brown spots and had the head of a benign and wise-looking giraffe.

"Tyson, if it's okay with your uncle, I can fix you up a little snack, some fruit or something, and I'll set up a TV tray for you in my living room. I've got a DVD you might like, or I can find some books for you to look at."

"That sounds like quite the deal, doesn't it, bud?" Paul said, keeping his attention on Tyson.

"It sure does!"

Paul helped Charlotte get Tyson settled, then they went to her kitchen and sat at the table.

"We should talk first," he said, "while Tyson is preoccupied."

"Yes, you said you wanted to talk to me about Mavis—and about Michael?"

Paul nodded but found that now that he

was here with her, it wasn't easy to put into words the overwhelming feeling that he had to approach things differently if he was going to be the kind of person who could live with himself.

"So, Tyson and Michael are really doing okay?" he asked, easing himself in on more familiar ground.

"Yes, they honestly are."

Paul shook his head. "I have to admit something to you. I'm kind of ashamed of myself," he blurted out.

Charlotte didn't answer with words, but her soft eyes urged him to continue, and he knew he could trust her not to judge him.

"Tyson has lost the people he needs most. He's only a little boy, but he's getting on with his life, he's not holding grudges and he's finding ways to genuinely enjoy himself again. How does he do that?"

"Maybe because he is a little boy," Charlotte suggested. "I know it's not easy to move on with life…" She stopped suddenly and asked, "Would you like tea or something?"

Paul shook his head. "No, thank you." He sensed that something had shifted in her, was sure he witnessed a fleeting but profound sadness, but was then just as sure that he must have imagined it.

"You said you wanted to talk about Mavis, too?" She got bottled water out of the fridge and sat down again.

As succinctly as he could, Paul told her how Mavis had brought her car to the garage, how he had recognized something was very wrong and how she ended up sobbing in his office.

"Her ex-husband is abusive," Paul concluded. "They've been trying to stay clear of him, but restraining orders don't always work as well as they should."

"I know," Charlotte said, grimly. "Or, at least, I suspected as much. Remember when I tried to talk to her at church? I saw that she had a bruise on her face."

Paul nodded. It was in Charlotte's nature to want to help someone, and he felt bad about his initial reaction to that.

"We talked a bit about Michael and Tyson," he continued. "She's sorry for the way Michael's been behaving, but at the same time…"

"She's protective of him," Charlotte agreed. "And she knows what's behind it."

"And now I know what's behind it, too."

"But it still isn't an excuse, is it?" Her eyes searched his.

He hesitated before answering, struggling

to find words that would encompass how he felt about the whole situation.

"No, it's not an excuse. I know how bullying can hurt and the emotional scars it leaves. But I think that what they've gone through is the worst kind of bullying, especially since it came at the hands of someone who was supposed to love and protect them."

"Did she say Michael was abused, too?" Charlotte asked anxiously.

"I don't think so, but it's had a severe impact on him, regardless."

They were silent for a moment, and suddenly into the silence came the incongruous burst of innocent laughter from the living room.

"It's because of you that Tyson is recovering so well," Charlotte said. "Don't ever forget that or sell yourself short."

"You've helped too," Paul said. "More than you know. You've been so good to both of us. You're a wonderful person, Charlotte."

As soon as he said the words, he knew that they meant more than just appreciation that she was Tyson's teacher, or that she was willing to help him learn how to read. It went much deeper than that. The timing might be all wrong for him to act on anything, but he couldn't stop himself from caring.

Her silence and the sweep of eyelashes on her flushed cheeks as she lowered her eyes spoke more loudly than any words could have. He knew beyond a doubt that Charlotte also felt the impact of his words.

He was seized with an almost overwhelming urge to kiss her. Not in the thoughtless, spontaneous way he had done at the school that day, but in a way that showed her that she mattered to him. He wanted to breathe in her clean soap smell and feel the silkiness of her hair sliding through his fingers. But Tyson was only a room away, and that wasn't why he had come here.

Charlotte cleared her throat, breaking the silence, which was beginning to feel unbearable, and took a sip of water. "So...what happens now? I mean, with Mavis," she hastily amended.

Paul snapped himself back to the matter at hand.

"I want to help her," he said.

"I thought you didn't like her," Charlotte said, trying to understand.

"I don't," Paul said bluntly. "But I'm not talking about being her best friend. I'm talking about doing the right thing and being the person that's good enough for my sister to have trusted to raise Tyson. I want to be a person he can be proud of."

He wanted Charlotte to be proud of him, too.

"I agree we should do something," Charlotte said. "The problem is that I don't know what we *can* do, other than let Mavis and Michael know that we're here if they ever need someone. I have to say I'm surprised she told you as much as she did."

"I think I was just at the right place and the right time. She's reached a breaking point, and I happened to be there to catch the pieces."

"I don't believe it was a coincidence," Charlotte said. "I think God placed you there for a reason. I know that you've been struggling with your beliefs, but..."

"I think so, too," Paul interjected softly.

Charlotte blinked, then her face opened up in a wide smile that tugged at his heart and made him wonder what it would be like to have someone he could share his faith and questions with.

"So, what do you think we should do?" Charlotte asked.

"That's why I wanted to talk to you," Paul said. "I want to hear your ideas." In the pause that followed, he realized that he hadn't heard Tyson's whoop of laugher in a few minutes.

"I'm just going to check on Ty," he said. "You know what they say about it being too quiet."

Charlotte laughed. "I do. I'm sure he's fine, but go ahead."

Paul went into Charlotte's living room. Tyson sat on the couch paging through what looked like a photo album.

"Hey, bud."

"Hi, Uncle Paul." The boy looked up with a placid expression.

"Where'd you get that? You know you probably shouldn't be looking at it without Ms. Connelly's permission."

"It was on the bottom here." Tyson pointed to the lower part of the coffee table.

"Okay, but we should ask Ms. Connelly if she minds you looking at it."

Paul followed his nephew back into the kitchen, where Charlotte waited with a thoughtful expression.

"Tyson came across a photo album you had sitting out," Paul said. "I thought he should ask you before going through it."

An expression that he couldn't decipher came over Charlotte's face. "Oh, I forgot I left that out..."

"Is this you, Ms. Connelly?" Tyson opened to a page and pointed. "It looks like you, but kinda different, too. Who's this girl with you? She kinda looks like you, too."

Charlotte felt like she was frozen in time, with the knowledge that the way she answered the question could change everything. She had never told anyone outside the family what had happened to Anna and why it was her fault. Her parents had wanted to carry on as best as they could, so Anna's name was rarely mentioned, even among themselves.

Except, Charlotte had felt for years that the secret sat like a cold, solid stone between her throat and heart—always there, always keeping her from living the fully purposeful life that she longed to live.

And now God had presented her with an opportunity to tell someone the truth, someone who she felt, for more than one reason, would understand. She had to choose: Was she going to take the chance, or was she going to stay afraid forever?

"That girl…was my sister, Anna," she heard her own voice say. She wanted to keep the words simple and direct for Tyson. "She died when she was ten years old."

She could feel rather than see Paul's reaction as his body stiffened.

Tyson put down the album and without a word crawled onto Charlotte's lap and hugged her. She closed her eyes and breathed in the smell of gingersnap cookies and bubblegum toothpaste.

"Tyson," Paul said very quietly. "Can you give Ms. Connelly and me a few minutes again?"

Tyson nodded and slid off his teacher's lap.

"I don't mind if you look at the pictures, Tyson," she said. "There are lots of happy memories there."

"You had a sister," Paul said when they were alone again, shaking his head slowly back and forth. "I can't believe I didn't know that. And you said she died when she was ten?" His eyes probed hers intently. "We've both lost a sister and you never said a thing?"

Charlotte understood that it wasn't an accusation, but that he was trying to understand.

"No one in town has said anything, either," he added.

Charlotte found her voice, or at least a semblance of it. "It's out of respect for us, for my family and me. My parents don't like to talk about Anna—or about what happened. Besides, there's no such thing as common grief," she added, thinking that surely, he of all people would realize that. "We may both have had sisters who died, but there was no appropriate time to bring up the subject, and even if I had, that doesn't mean we feel the same way about it. At least…" Was she really going to say it out loud?

Dear God, please give me the strength to stop hiding.

"Your sister's death was a terrible tragedy, but at least it wasn't your fault."

Paul beckoned her to move her chair closer to his. He took both of her hands in his large, warm ones and in a voice more quiet and gentle than she could have imagined coming out of a man his size, he said, "Tell me what happened. Please."

And so she told him the story of a lake and a summer cabin that had once meant the heady freedom of summer to her and her family, but how all of that ended when she was fifteen and was supposed to be watching her younger sister out in the lake, but let the giddy adventure of flirting with a cute boy distract her just long enough for all of their lives to change forever.

"As long as I live," Charlotte said, in an empty, brittle voice, "I know I will never forget being walked back up to our cabin so I could tell my parents what happened…what I had done."

Paul let go of her hands, and for a moment she believed he was abandoning her as she surely deserved. But then he was pulling her into his arms and murmuring into her hair, "It wasn't your fault. It was an accident, a terrible accident."

After so many years, she was finally able to let go of the knot that had been coiled up in her like a poisonous snake for years. She sobbed in Paul's arms, deep and painful but profoundly cleansing sobs. And all the while he made soothing noises and she became aware of his lips kissing her hair and her forehead. His strong arms sheltered her, providing a feeling of incredible safety.

"Shhh," he whispered. "It's going to be all right. Shhh."

A rustle coming from the living room caught her attention and she reluctantly drew back.

"Ty-Tyson," she choked.

Paul laughed then, a rueful chuckle, and took his own step back. There was deep compassion and a light of something else in his eyes that caused her heart to beat out a response.

"Yeah, I should get him," he said, but he didn't take his eyes off her.

"We didn't get anything done," Charlotte said, regretfully.

"Yes," Paul said. "We did."

Slowly, he bent his head toward her, searching her eyes, perhaps for permission—but she knew that he was asking for more than permission to kiss her; he was asking her if he could take the secret she'd shared and use it as a bridge to a deeper connection.

And suddenly it felt like the years-old prayer that she'd hardly been able to find words for did have an answer: she could stay here—there were people here like Mavis and Michael and the newcomers at the community center who needed her. She had trusted Paul with her most shameful secret, and he had stayed. Not only had he stayed, he was showing her that he cared, deeply. Every part of her believed that God was telling her that she could have it all: she could have purpose in life, she could be there for her family and she could explore the possibility of a deepening relationship with Paul Belvedere.

She went up on her tiptoes and initiated the kiss herself. She kissed him and felt the strength of his arms tightening around her, his lips gentle against hers. She kept kissing him, almost overwhelmed by a sense of relief and homecoming. She kissed him with all of her heart.

Chapter Twenty

It was really quite amazing, Paul thought, the way the letters C-A-T could conjure up the picture of a fluffy feline sleeping contentedly by the fireplace. That is, until the D-O-G came to chase him away.

What was more remarkable, though, was that he finally felt like he was in a place he could call home, with the most wonderful best friend to help him make the transition into committed, small-town guy.

He and Charlotte seemed to both understand without words that the kiss, as heart-skippingly wonderful as it was, signified their trust in one another: he had shared his greatest secret with her, and she had not betrayed him, and now she had shared hers with him and he planned to honor her trust with every fiber of him. But it still felt like a romance was both too simplistic and too complicated to encompass what they shared. So, in the meantime, he would treasure Charlotte, in all of her dimensions, and he would thank God—and mean it—for helping him believe that happiness was possible again.

Things at the community center were going well, too. He had added confidence now, when they taught the fix-it class, because he was working hard behind the scenes to improve his reading. It gave him a particularly strong empathy for what the newcomers went through in learning the language of their new country, and the lessons had become a time of openness, laughter and sharing.

It had been a while since Charlotte had mentioned going overseas. Sometimes the question of it would briefly itch under Paul's skin and stir through the pit of his stomach. But surely she would mention it if that was still her intention, and these days she had a restfulness and contentment that matched his.

They continued to share the goal of helping Mavis and Michael, which wasn't an easy thing to do. After her confession to him in her frightened and broken moment, Mavis had become more elusive and skittish than ever. If either he or Charlotte ever ran into her directly, it was like a cloak made of iron dropped over her, making her hard and impenetrable.

But at least Michael was at school and Charlotte could keep an eye on him there.

One Sunday morning, Paul went to wake Tyson up for church and found his nephew already sitting up in bed with an eager face.

"This is really getting to be part of our sked-you-all, isn't it, Uncle Paul?" he asked.

Paul chuckled. "What are you doing, talking about schedules at your age? And yes, it sure is."

"I bet my mom and my dad are happy we're going to church."

Paul swallowed, but the lump of grief was now seasoned by the passage of time and went down a bit easier.

It was hard to believe that soon it would be November. Tyson and Max's long-wished-for snow was in the forecast.

"Yes, I believe they are," he answered Tyson. He no longer felt bitter when his nephew said things like that.

Tyson suddenly hurled himself into his uncle's arms for a hug.

"Me and Max and Michael are all gonna sit together and do our project," he announced. "We don't know what it's gonna be yet, but we already decided we'll do it together." He didn't appear to think there was anything extraordinary in that fact, but just accepted that things had changed and what had happened before didn't matter anymore.

Paul mused that there was a good lesson in that.

"Come have breakfast," he urged.

"It's eggs and bacon, right?" That had become their Sunday tradition.

"Sure is, bud, and you'd better get there quick before I grab all the crispy pieces."

"No way!" Tyson jumped out of bed and hurried down the stairs.

"Careful!" Paul called after him.

After breakfast, while Tyson was getting dressed, Paul studied his own collection of shirts in his closet, trying to find one that Charlotte had said she liked the color of. He looked forward to hearing the next part of the sermon series on the Book of James. It wasn't easy to think that people could find joy in their trials, but he was especially interested in what the pastor had to say on the matter, as it gave him things to ponder on his own journey toward trust.

Then he shook his head, laughing at himself. He couldn't accept the profound changes his life had undergone quite as readily as Tyson did, but he was thankful for them.

The day was sunny and crisp and leaves in a glorious array of colors lay on lawns and sidewalks. Paul urged Tyson to keep hold of his hand, but sometimes a sheer burst of joy and abandonment would overtake Tyson and he would let go of his uncle's hand and dance ahead a few steps. Once he caught the toe of his shoe on a curb and he almost stumbled, causing Paul to hold his breath, but he managed to right himself and turned back with a proud grin.

He's not afraid of falling because he knows he'll survive it.

As soon as they entered the church, Tyson skipped off to find his friends. Paul knew his nephew was comfortable and safe in the church, and he no longer felt compelled to worry about him when he was out of sight. He had to admit that it was a relief to let go of the chronic feeling of responsibility. Not in the way that dismissed his love for Tyson, but in the way that he was finally learning to accept that others could also play a part in making sure his nephew had a happy and secure life.

The foyer of the church was crowded, as always, with visiting before the service. Instead of avoiding it, Paul found he now enjoyed sharing a few words with various people. Always, though, he kept his eye out for Charlotte, because she was never far from his thoughts.

"I checked my car oil," a voice said shyly at his shoulder, and he turned to see one of the members of his fix-it class, her deep brown eyes shining with quiet pride. "Just like you said to do, I checked."

"That's great!" Paul said, giving the woman a high five, which made her giggle. "I knew you could do it."

Across the room, he caught a glimpse of Olivia Meissner watching. She didn't smile, but she gave him a brief nod, which he returned.

Then he spotted Charlotte. Today, her hair curled softly around her shoulders, against the robin egg's blue of her sweater. She was saying something to her mother and hadn't seen him yet. Before he could catch her eye, she turned in the other direction to head downstairs and check on the Sunday school rooms as she sometimes liked to do.

Disappointment briefly assailed him before he reminded himself that he would get a chance to talk to her later. It occurred to him that it would be the polite thing to do to go greet her parents. He wasn't particularly comfortable around them and wondered where Charlotte managed to get her warmth and compassion, as he found George and Lenore Connelly rather cool and distant. But they were Charlotte's parents, and now that he knew about the tragic loss they'd endured, he could imagine that a depth of feeling dwelled beneath their aloof exteriors. Charlotte had said that they didn't like to talk about it, but surely it wouldn't hurt to offer his condolences. Surely they would know that he, of all people, could empathize with their pain.

"Good morning, Lenore, George," Paul greeted them as he approached.

"Oh." Lenore hesitated slightly before answering. "Hello, Paul. How are you this morning?"

"I'm really good, thanks." He hesitated, relying on God to help him find the words. "I wondered if you had just a moment before we go in?"

Lenore's eyes flickered with puzzlement and perhaps a glimmer of unease. George came to stand beside his wife and put his hand on her shoulder in what seemed like a cautioning rather than an affectionate gesture.

"I haven't had a chance to tell you how

very sorry I was to hear about your daughter Anna," he said.

Lenore's eyes widened in a clearly appalled manner while George's hand clenched her shoulder in a way that made Paul wince, although she didn't even seem aware of it.

When she found her voice, it was like it had been torn to shreds. "Charlotte told you about Anna?"

He realized that he had made a colossal error in judgment, but he had no choice now but to carry on. "Yes…she did. You know I lost my sister and brother-in-law? I don't mean to upset you. I just wanted you to know that I understand."

"I appreciate your thoughts, Paul," Lenore said in a voice that was all the more terrible for its flatness. "But it's not something we wish to discuss with you. I'm sorry for your own loss, I truly am."

Then she regained herself and said to her husband, "Shall we go in?"

"I know you meant well," George said quietly to Paul as his wife went in ahead of him. "But you've upset my wife, and I thank you not to ever do that again. Do you understand?"

Paul nodded. He understood. And he was beginning to understand how hard it must be on Charlotte to not be allowed to grieve. He longed to console her and help her as much as he was capable of, although he knew that it was ultimately a journey that one did alone.

Stephanie, who was teaching Sunday school that week, had accidentally mixed up the schedule for the week's lesson and didn't have the proper materials prepared, so Charlotte stayed to assist her in setting things up and was slightly late getting back upstairs. She slid in beside her mother during the opening song and received a fretful sideways glance in greeting.

Paul had developed the habit of sitting behind them, and she sought an opportunity to try to see if he was there without making it obvious that she was looking. She resigned herself that she might have to wait until later in the service when the peace was shared. But as the song ended and the waiting silence settled over the congregation, she had a peculiar sense of emptiness that told her that Paul wasn't there. She also noticed that her parents seemed distracted and troubled about something, which ruined the restful feeling she usually had at church.

She couldn't stop her mind from wandering and she couldn't even bring herself to concentrate enough to take sermon notes, as she usually liked to do. Usually, the Sunday morning service sped by, but the time seem to drag. When they shared the peace, she confirmed for herself that Paul wasn't behind them. As she shook hands and forced a smile, she spotted him across the aisle, sitting with Sean and Rena.

He was certainly welcome to sit where he wanted, but it bothered her that he had moved to a different pew on the same day that her parents were clearly troubled about something.

She didn't have to wait long to find out what troubled her mother and father. As soon as the closing song ended, Lenore took her elbow and murmured in her ear, "We need to talk to you." She kept her hand on Charlotte's elbow, and Charlotte felt herself being steered efficiently toward the coatrack.

Curious about what was on their minds, Charlotte followed her parents out. When they had put some distance between themselves and the church, her mother turned to her and said, "So, you decided to share our family tragedy with Paul? With someone we hardly know?"

"I do know Paul!" flew out of Charlotte's mouth. She didn't bother to deny that she had told him about Anna. Obviously he had said something to them about it. Well, she hadn't specifically told him not to, but then something fierce and defiant welled up in her.

Why can't we talk about it ourselves, God? I believe that keeping this bottled up is hurting all of us, and it's not honoring Anna's memory. I'm asking You to help us break free of this.

Out loud, she said as calmly as she could manage. "I think it's okay to talk about Anna. I think we *have* to talk about her…and about what happened."

"We just think that it doesn't do any good to dwell on it, Charlotte," her father said. "I would think you would feel the same way. Your mother and I have never wanted you to hold on to the memory of that tragic day."

"I would think," she said very quietly, with her heart in pieces, "that I of all people would need to talk about it so I can forgive myself."

And then in one dreadful instant Charlotte knew that nothing here was ever going to change. Perhaps it was the heady experience of Paul's kiss that had caused her to believe that it was possible to stay in Green Valley and have everything she ever dreamed of.

But she knew now that wasn't true and she believed now that it never would be true. There was no other answer: if she was ever going to find healing for herself, it would have to be away from home... Even if that meant leaving Paul Belvedere behind.

Chapter Twenty-One

Another Wednesday night at the church was wrapping up and Paul, along with Joe, Seth and Harold, was busy stacking chairs and moving tables back into place.

Charlotte's teaching methods, along with learning the basics, were working wonders and it was truly amazing to pick up a tool and see the name for it take shape in his mind. He felt like he had a new lease on life, so he not only enjoyed teaching his class but now also felt like he had the self-confidence to enjoy the fellowship that came before and after.

He no longer felt like his secret burdened him the way it always had.

But he also knew that everything he felt was enhanced by the way he felt about Charlotte. She was like a beacon, shining light on his days, encouraging him to continue to build his trust in God, and in his own innate abilities to learn and improve. Tyson adored her, which was an added bonus.

She had helped with the group alongside him, as she always did, although she was more quiet than usual and seemed sad in a way that he couldn't pinpoint. But he didn't worry the way he might have in the past. He would talk to her and find out what was on her mind.

Besides, the fact that God was always with him and he was never really abandoned had struck him with a new and profound conviction. Charlotte was part of that, too. It often happened that as they worked around her house, with her literally spelling out things, she would talk about her faith, not in an overly preachy way, but like she and God were friends and she couldn't imagine her life without Him.

He found himself wanting that same intimacy with the Lord.

"See you tomorrow, Paul." Harold gave a wave as he headed out the door.

"Sure thing."

"There you are!" Rena came into the room. "Come on, Seth. We've got two episodes of that mystery show you like to catch up on."

"Sorry, gentlemen, duty calls." Seth said. "It's a rough job, but somebody has to do it."

Rena rolled her eyes but held out her hand for him to take.

"Is Charlotte still around?" Paul asked. She had left their classroom as soon as they were finished, and he'd gotten caught up answering a couple of extra questions and lost track of her.

Rena turned her twinkling gaze on him. "Yes, she should be. I saw her just a few minutes ago with Steph, putting books away."

Paul nodded, trying to suppress his urge to rush off and find her. He wished Seth and Rena a good night and turned back to Joe to see if there was anything else that needed to be done.

"I think we're good here, thanks," Joe said. "Catch you around."

Paul located Tyson first, playing with Max while her parents chatted with Eugenie in the doorway. "I just have to go talk to someone for a few minutes," Paul told Eugenie. "I won't be long."

"No worries," Eugenie said.

"Take your time, Uncle Paul!" Tyson called after him.

By the time he got to the literacy room, it was empty, and he spotted Stephanie with her coat on, heading out the door. He was momentarily resigned to not seeing Charlotte that night, but then he spotted her by the coat-track with Bridget. Their heads were bowed close together, and they appeared to be involved in an intense conversation.

Bridget must have sensed that he was there, because she looked over suddenly and gave him a quick smile and wave before turning back to Charlotte to say something else. Soon after, she put on her coat and departed, leaving Charlotte standing alone.

"How are you doing?" Paul asked as he approached her. When he got close enough, he noticed that her beautiful violet eyes looked troubled. "What's wrong, Charlotte?"

She looked down and toyed with a button at the neckline of the cream-colored, rose-sprigged blouse that she wore.

"Char, is everything okay?" Paul felt the old tide of apprehension rise up within him, the pool of old emotions and hurt that he'd thought was finally drying up. Now he feared that it was just waiting to seep through the chronic cracks of life.

She looked him full in the eye then, her expression sad and thoughtful.

"I...have something that I need to tell you."

"Oh?" He heard his own voice go cold and distancing, trying to push away her power to hurt him.

"I don't know how to say it because, honestly, Paul, you mean so much to me—you and Tyson—I'm so grateful for what we've shared. I hope you know that…"

"Just. Say. It." His voice sliced through her preamble like a sword.

Her head reeled slightly back as if she felt the sting of its tip. Then she steadied herself and said, in her teacher voice, "I'm going away. I've decided that I am going to take the overseas missionary opportunity."

"When the school year is over?" Paul asked, plucking that question out of the plethora of them that raced through his mind.

Again, Charlotte hesitated. When she answered, her voice wavered between defiance and regret. "No. I'm going after Christmas. They're finding someone to take over my class."

Hurt and anger ripped through Paul like a bullet. He didn't know if he was more upset with Charlotte, with God, or with himself for actually being foolish enough to believe that things would ever really change.

"What about Tyson?" The question barely scratched the surface of the ones that he was yearning to ask—*What about me? What about us?*—but it was all he could manage. "I thought you promised that he'd be able to finish out the school year with the same teacher. What about that?"

Charlotte looked at her feet and whispered, "I'm sorry. I thought I could stay, but I can't."

Silence pulsed between them, heavy with things that needed to be said—things that felt like they could never be said.

"Charlotte…" Paul put one finger under her chin and gently coaxed her gaze upward to his face. "I'm asking you not to go. Please, don't go."

Long seconds passed and it was like watching a drama of fear, sadness and indecision play through her eyes. But then the reel snapped before the ending.

Charlotte took a step back from him.

"I have to go," she said. "I can't live my life under other people's expectations anymore. I can't live wondering 'what if.' I'm going."

He took a step back, too. "I guess that's it, then."

"Paul, I still want to help you with your reading. Until I go… We have plenty of time."

"No," he said. "We don't have enough time at all."

Without another word, he turned and walked away.

* * *

On Friday at lunchtime, Charlotte sat in the staff room with a mug of chamomile tea clutched in her hands, but she had no interest in it, or in the ham and cheese on rye that lay untouched on the table.

She had just finished unburdening herself to Rena. Since confiding in Paul about Anna, she'd found that there was freedom in confession. Something that God, through His word, definitely encouraged. She told Rena about Anna, about her parents' expectations and about her growing relationship with Paul—one that was now halted by her decision to go away.

Rena sat across from her, her brown eyes sympathetic over her own mug as she took a sip of coffee. "I think you have to follow your heart," she said. "If Paul's truly a friend, he'll get over it and support you."

"He is a good friend," Charlotte said, feeling an instant need to defend him. There was so much more she knew about Paul now, and she understood why he felt abandoned, which made her decision excruciating. But those things were his own burdens to share if he chose, and she would not betray his trust.

"Do your parents know you're going?" Rena asked.

Charlotte shook her head. "I'm going to tell them at dinner tonight. Bridget and her parents will be there, too. I might as well get over telling them all at once. Bridget doesn't want me to go, either. She thinks I'm letting my family down. And, of course, everyone is worried about my mom's health. I am, too, but…"

Rena traced her fingertip around the table-top, making circles. "But you still have to go, don't you?"

Charlotte didn't answer right away. Finally she said, "I'm tired of letting myself down. I always say that I want to make a difference, but what have I done to show that I mean it?"

"You make a difference here."

Charlotte shrugged. "I guess so. But it still feels like if I stay here, something will always get in the way of me living the life I want to live."

"But what if that life *is* here?" Rena asked. "I'm not trying to talk you out of going. I fully support you, you know that. I'm just trying to help you consider all of the angles. What if everything you want really is right here?"

And everyone? Charlotte asked silently. She thought about the moment of elation she'd had when she believed it was possible to have it all…and how quickly and devastatingly that belief had been punctured.

"I appreciate what you're saying, Rena, but I can't see that happening."

After lunch, she returned to her classroom and by sheer willpower guided her students through their art project. She noted that Tyson and Michael had their heads bent together, whispering, and she noted that God still could fix some things, but it seemed that He would pick and choose.

She kept trying to bolster herself, telling herself that she was finally following her dreams, going in the direction that she was called in. But she couldn't help wondering that if she was truly called, why was the voice so distant and faint? Why did it keep fading away under her wish to stay? But if she stayed, nothing would change. The conflict chased itself around in her mind like a rabid hound chasing a rabbit, and it would not resolve itself.

Mildred came to pick up Tyson—a fact that didn't completely surprise Charlotte but disappointed her all the same.

She kept her smile bright as she ushered child after child into the care of whoever was picking them up. Michael still sat at his desk, reading a book. Mavis was often late, so it didn't worry Charlotte, though she was anxious to be alone with her thoughts. She knew Mavis would dart her head into the classroom just long enough to let her son know she was there, and Michael would quickly gather his belongings and hurry out.

Charlotte never had found out why Mavis was trying to track her down. She imagined it was because of the recess incident, but clearly things that had pressed into Mavis's life overshadowed it. For today, at least, Charlotte was just as glad that the other woman had nothing to say to her. She was anxious to be alone and to ask God one more time to reassure her that she was doing the right thing.

But, once again, it appeared that God had other plans.

When Mavis showed up, she startled Charlotte by asking, "Can I talk to you?" Mavis hovered at her desk with her arms awkwardly hanging at her sides.

"Of course. How can I help you?" Charlotte asked, pulling out every molecule of professional decorum that she had. She hoped that Mavis would at least have the sense not to have it out with her in front of her son.

"You wrote in Michael's art book that you love the way he draws birds," she blurted out.

"I did," Charlotte agreed. "And I meant it. Michael has a wonderful eye. He notices things."

"Most people just think he's bad all the time. They don't know…" Mavis's voice faltered, then she braced herself, and when she spoke, her voice sounded even harsher, but Charlotte could hear the pain within it.

"They don't know…it hurts to have people misunderstand—not to know what your life is all about."

"I know," Charlotte said. "And I think everyone has something good in them."

"Well, I think you're good at helping people find that," Mavis said. "It's got me thinking that maybe I'm the one who has to figure out what's good and what works instead of running all the time. Thank you for that." Then she barked out a scornful laugh as if she was ashamed of herself for being vulnerable. "Let's go, Mikey. I haven't got all day."

For a long time after they left, Charlotte sat at her desk, pondering.

God…? Did You…?

Because maybe, just maybe, He had answered her question using the most unexpected source possible; because He was God and because He could do whatever He wanted.

But the longer she sat there and thought

about what Mavis had said about not running, the more she realized that there was nothing she could do, whether she stayed or left, to change the tragic fact that Anna had drowned. As she realized that she was responsible for her own healing, she finally realized that her parents were responsible for theirs. Going away wouldn't truly solve anything, at least not if she left feeling the way that she did. She had to confront them, and she had to tell them that she would no longer allow them to hold her hostage to their own guilt and remorse.

She lifted her head and, with her eyes streaming with tears but her heart full of new determination, she thanked God for finally showing her the way.

Chapter Twenty-Two

"Is everything okay, Paul?" Harold asked as they prepared to close shop on Friday.

"Did I do something wrong?" Paul asked.

"Of course not," Harold said. "I'm not asking about work, I'm asking about you."

Paul thought that it was rather a shame that this town continually showed its kindness and concern to him and Tyson but still couldn't deliver what he wanted most of all: a future with a certain person who couldn't wait to get away.

He had done everything he could to avoid Charlotte since they'd parted on Wednesday. That meant asking Mildred to pick up Tyson from school. He felt bad about that, but he didn't see that he had another choice.

As for his reading, he battled down the feeling that you never knew what you were missing until you lost it. He'd gotten along okay without it so far and he was determined that he would continue to do so.

Except for knowing that he'd gained and lost much more than learning to read…

He realized that he hadn't answered Harold.

"I'm okay, thanks for asking. It's just been, ah, kind of a tough week."

"Anything you want to talk about?"

"I appreciate the offer, but no."

Paul left work, and as he headed toward Mildred's house to pick up Tyson, he kept up a silent debate with God.

Somewhat to his own surprise, his disappointment in Charlotte hadn't caused him to stop talking to God. Instead, his prayers grew more intense than ever. He thought about the way she talked about finding solace in His word, and he couldn't help wondering if there were Scriptures that could help him deal with how he was feeling. But how would he ever know?

Ask for help.

The thought literally stopped him in his tracks.

Thoughts and questions continued to barrage his mind and heart. What would he accomplish if he continued to keep his secret? What would he risk by telling it? What would he lose by not?

The realization dawned that whether he learned to read or not and what he did with his future was his alone to make. No matter how much he cared for Charlotte and hoped she cared for him, she wasn't responsible for his future or for his happiness, and it wasn't fair for him to hold her back.

He had to find her. He had to tell her.

Charlotte laid her fork down beside what was left of her strawberry rhubarb pie. She told herself, *It's now or never*, and gave a silent prayer. Yet somehow she already knew that God was with her and that He'd only been waiting for her to realize what she had to do.

"We're going to talk about Anna," she began in a firm voice.

Immediately, it was like the actual air around the table changed, filled with gazes that were either averted or filled with pain.

But she didn't waver.

"I am deeply sorry for my role in what happened. But I was fifteen years old. If I could go back and change what happened, I would, but I can't. All I can do is move forward and remember Anna the way she deserves to be remembered. And I've decided that's what I'm going to do. I'm going to talk about her when I want to, and remember things about her, and laugh about what a funny little girl she was."

She paused and looked pleadingly at her father and her mother, who was hugging her own stomach.

She looked at them and she loved them with her whole heart, but she knew she couldn't make things better for them…nor was she expected to.

"I love all of you," she said, glancing around the table. Bridget met her gaze directly, her mouth trembling, but she nodded and attempted a smile.

Finally her mother answered. "We love you, too, Charlotte." Her father nodded.

Charlotte was happy to hear it, but she no longer expected them to change. Her parents had their own journey to travel, and she had made her peace with God and with herself.

And now she was ready to tell Paul that she was staying. Not because he or anyone else demanded it of her, but because she no longer had to run.

* * *

Later that evening, Paul and Tyson stood outside Charlotte's house. Paul rang the doorbell, then rang it again.

"She's not home," Tyson said.

"I guess not." Paul tried to keep the disappointment out of his voice. "Well, since we're out anyway, should we get some hot chocolate at Seth's?"

Tyson bounced along beside him. "Yeah!"

They were halfway there when they spotted Charlotte heading in their direction.

"Ms. Connelly!" Tyson bolted in her direction. "We were just at your house."

"You were?" she smiled absently at him, but her eyes sought out Paul.

"I had to see you," Paul said. "To tell you that I'm sorry, and that I realized that if I truly love you, I won't stop you from doing what makes you happy."

Beneath the streetlight, Charlotte's eyes shone. "I was looking for you, too," she said. "I wanted to tell you that I'm going to stay and that…" She stopped. "You love me?"

Paul nodded. "You're staying? Does that mean that…?"

"I love you, too, Paul. I want us to have a life here. I want us to make a difference here, together."

They embraced while Tyson jumped around them and asked, "Can Ms. Connelly come have hot chocolate with us?"

Paul smoothed a strand of hair behind her ear and whispered, "Do you think Tyson should practice calling you Aunt Charlotte?"

He gave one hand to Charlotte, the other to Tyson, and together they moved forward.

Epilogue

"You look so lovely, Charlotte, dear," her mother said as she adjusted the white silk flower in Charlotte's hair. It was a crisp and sunny day the following September.

Charlotte had not wanted a dress that was too frothy or overwhelming, and the simple but elegant lines of the white lace gown she wore suited her perfectly.

"You do look so beautiful, Char," Bridget reaffirmed in an awed voice. She and Rena wore matching silk bridesmaid dresses in autumn shades of gold and coral.

"I can't believe this day is finally here," Charlotte said. "It still doesn't feel quite real."

Less than a year ago, she had barely known Paul Belvedere. And now, on this warm morning in September, with the trees beginning to change their wardrobes to yellow, red and brown, she was about to become his wife.

Tyson had entered grade two with confidence and enthusiasm. If he had any regrets about not being in Ms. Connelly's class anymore, being able to call her Aunt Charlotte instead more than made up for it.

Since Paul and Tyson had come into her life, she continued to learn what God was capable of.

"I wish that..." Charlotte began to say, then stopped.

"I wish Anna was here, too," Lenore finished for her.

Charlotte swallowed and hugged her mother.

It had taken time, but after she had confronted her parents with her need to talk openly about Anna, they were finally facing their own grief. Her mother had sought counseling to help her with the process and her physical symptoms were improving.

"Anna is here in our hearts and our memories," Charlotte said.

George poked his head in. "There's a young man down the hall who's getting anxious to see his bride. And who can blame him? You look absolutely wonderful, Charlotte."

Down the church hallway in another room, Paul adjusted his bow tie and checked his reflection in the mirror. He thought his black tuxedo looked all right, but mostly what he saw was his eyes glowing with anticipation.

"I'm happy for you, Paul," Seth said. "You and Charlotte are perfect together."

Tyson, dressed in his own tuxedo and bow tie, stalked around the room with his hands bent into claws in front of him. "I'm the ring bear. Grrrr!"

Instead of telling him it was ring *bearer*, Paul scooped him into a hug. "How about a bear hug for the ring bear?"

Tyson wriggled and snorted with laughter.

"Ready to get me married to Ms. Connelly?" Paul asked.

"She's not Ms. Connelly anymore," Tyson corrected. "She's Auntie Charlotte."

The music began. They stepped out of the room and waited at the front of the church.

Paul felt like his heart couldn't possibly hold any more happiness, as he watched his beautiful bride walk down the aisle toward him on her father's arm.

The minister gave a warm welcome to the congregation. Then he said, "Before we get to the vows and the exchange of the rings, Paul has asked for time to share his thoughts with his bride."

A murmur of joyful anticipation stirred

through the congregation, as Paul's best man handed him a folded piece of paper. But his eyes were locked on the beautiful violet eyes of the woman he loved—the woman he intended to spend the rest of his life with.

His hands trembled a bit with emotion and nerves, then Charlotte's loving and encouraging smile calmed him and he unfolded the paper and began to read the words that he had written just for her: "Charlotte," he began, his voice filled with emotion, "When I came into your classroom that first day, I had no idea that God would use you to change me, to help me let go of the fear I had, and that I would find love with you…"

With God's help, Paul knew, they would continue to love, trust and help one another grow to be the best people they could be as they faced the future together with open hearts.

* * * * *

If you enjoyed Instant Father,
look for Donna Gartshore's earlier book

Instant Family

Available now from Love Inspired!

Find more great reads at
www.LoveInspired.com

Dear Reader,

Thank you so much for reading *Instant Father* and spending time with Paul, Charlotte and Tyson.

Being people of faith doesn't always stop us from doubting ourselves and feeling like we must hide our flaws from others. It also doesn't stop us from letting the expectations of others influence our decisions.

Both Paul and Charlotte struggle with these things and it is only by learning that they can trust God to be strong in their weaknesses that they are willing to take a chance on each other and on love.

I wrote this book because I wished to express that, although we are imperfect, God loves us and we can all have fulfilling lives. We do not need to let our shortcomings define us.

I also brought bullying into the story because I believe it's an ongoing issue that we all need to be aware of, pray about and take a stand against.

I know I speak for all Love Inspired authors when I say that our readers mean the world to us. We are so thankful that you read our books and we love to engage with you.

Please join our Love Inspired Author and Reader Group on Facebook. We want to connect with you, pray with and for you, and hear about your lives.

I can also be reached via email at deelynn1000@hotmail.com; friend me or like my author page on Facebook; follow me on Twitter @gartshoredonna or on Instagram @dlgwrites.

Thank you again from the bottom of my heart and I look forward to hearing from you!

Blessings,
Donna Gartshore

Get 4 FREE REWARDS!

We'll send you 2 FREE Books <u>plus</u> 2 FREE Mystery Gifts.

Love Inspired® Suspense books feature Christian characters facing challenges to their faith... and lives.

FREE Value Over **$20**

YES! Please send me 2 FREE Love Inspired® Suspense novels and my 2 FREE mystery gifts (gifts are worth about $10 retail). After receiving them, if I don't wish to receive any more books, I can return the shipping statement marked "cancel." If I don't cancel, I will receive 4 brand-new novels every month and be billed just $5.24 each for the regular-print edition or $5.74 each for the larger-print edition in the U.S., or $5.74 each for the regular-print edition or $6.24 each for the larger-print edition in Canada. That's a savings of at least 13% off the cover price. It's quite a bargain! Shipping and handling is just 50¢ per book in the U.S. and 75¢ per book in Canada.* I understand that accepting the 2 free books and gifts places me under no obligation to buy anything. I can always return a shipment and cancel at any time. The free books and gifts are mine to keep no matter what I decide.

Choose one: ☐ **Love Inspired® Suspense Regular-Print** (153/353 IDN GMY5)   ☐ **Love Inspired® Suspense Larger-Print** (107/307 IDN GMY5)

Name (please print)

Address   Apt. #

City   State/Province   Zip/Postal Code

Mail to the **Reader Service:**
IN U.S.A.: P.O. Box 1341, Buffalo, NY 14240-8531
IN CANADA: P.O. Box 603, Fort Erie, Ontario L2A 5X3

Want to try 2 free books from another series? Call 1-800-873-8635 or visit www.ReaderService.com.

Get 4 FREE REWARDS!

We'll send you 2 FREE Books
<u>plus</u> 2 FREE Mystery Gifts.

Harlequin® Heartwarming™ Larger-Print books feature traditional values of home, family, community and—most of all—love.

FREE Value Over **$20**

YES! Please send me 2 FREE Harlequin® Heartwarming™ Larger-Print novels and my 2 FREE mystery gifts (gifts worth about $10 retail). After receiving them, if I don't wish to receive any more books, I can return the shipping statement marked "cancel." If I don't cancel, I will receive 4 brand-new larger-print novels every month and be billed just $5.49 per book in the U.S. or $6.24 per book in Canada. That's a savings of at least 19% off the cover price. It's quite a bargain! Shipping and handling is just 50¢ per book in the U.S. and 75¢ per book in Canada.* I understand that accepting the 2 free books and gifts places me under no obligation to buy anything. I can always return a shipment and cancel at any time. The free books and gifts are mine to keep no matter what I decide.

161/361 IDN GMY3

Name (please print)

Address   Apt. #

City   State/Province   Zip/Postal Code

Mail to the Reader Service:
IN U.S.A.: P.O. Box 1341, Buffalo, NY 14240-8531
IN CANADA: P.O. Box 603, Fort Erie, Ontario L2A 5X3

Want to try 2 free books from another series? Call 1-800-873-8635 or visit www.ReaderService.com.